The Anointed Assassins by
Isaac Gavin

PRELUDE

Caught between a hard place and a rock with the walls closing in Caller needs a way out. Because he no longer sees his world through the same lens as he did when he organized his hit squad. He wants to end it but his comrades want to continue until every last one of their intended targets are eliminated. If they find out that he is no longer committed to their original goal and is communicating with an adversary (news reporter) who could be detrimental to their goals, then Caller and his family and the reporter could be their next target. Time is running out and other targets are in the crosshairs.

Copyrighted © 2019 Isaac Gavin
All rights reserved.
No part of this publication may be reproduced,
distributed or transmitted in any form or by
any means.

This book is dedicated to Rashad, Nya, Kai, my Grandmother Julia Gavin, who taught me to "trust and obey."

Isaac Gavin

Contents

Part 1. Genesis

- The Beginning
- Choices We Make
- Symbols Of Justice
- Who, What, When, Where, And Why
- The Good, The Bad, And Law Enforcement
- Talk To Me
- Meeting Of The Minds
- All Hell Breaks Loose

Part 2. Five Smooth Stones

- The Punisher
- The God I Never Knew
- Wade In The Water
- Light Inside The Darkness
- Dis-Connecting The Dots
- No More Secrets

Part 3. At The Red Sea

- Saved By The Bell

- Coming In From The Rain
- Anonymous
- I Have A Dream
- Somebody Is Watching You
- Am I My Brother's Keeper
- Back In The Game
- Family Matters
- Candid Camera

Part 4. David vs Goliath

- The Walls Of Jericho
- Judge, Jury, And Executioner
- The Good Shepherd
- Here We Go Again
- A Helping Hand
- Facing Giants
- Verity And Justice
- Angels And Demons
- Faith Or Fiction
- Here Comes The Pain

Part 5. Exodus

- It's A Wonderful Life
- Let Your Conscious Be Your Guide
- The Untouchables
- The Court Of Public Opinion
- Now You Hear Me Now You Don't
- Come Out, Come Out, Where Ever You Are
- It's A Wonderful Day In The Neighborhood

Part 1. Genesis

"Sometimes we walk in the light and sometimes we walk in the dark...faith and hope helps us to keep moving forward putting one foot in front of the other" IG

The Beginning

It was a cool evening and darkness had just begun to set in over the city. There was a light breeze blowing and you could hear the leaves rustling in the trees. I thought to myself, another Autumn in the city of cities, New York, the big apple. Yes, New York City was known as the big apple, but crooked politicians and judges, and those sworn to uphold and enforce the law had started this apple to rot from the core.

As I turned the corner on the street where I lived for the past five years suddenly I heard popping sounds like fireworks on the fourth of July. I lived in the Upper West Manhattan neighborhood where there was an abundance of yuppies, such as lawyers, doctors, judges, politicians and other professionals.

It was a clear night and the moon shone bright and full.

Suddenly I heard the sound of a woman screaming. The screams were coming from a parking garage that I had just walk past. A part of me wanted to turn around and enter the garage to see what had just happened but fear got the best of me and because I was now just across the street from my apartment I decided not to turn around and go back.

As I got closer to my building I looked over my shoulder and I could see the image of someone running from the direction of the parking garage. The screams of the woman voice grew louder and louder. I was about to put my key in the door of my building when I heard the woman cry out, help, someone please, help me. Something inside of me wanted the go in the direction of the screams, but knowing that the sounds I just heard were likely gun shots and not fireworks persuaded me not to.

Suddenly there was the sound of tires screeching and out of the darkness a black SUV appeared and turned the corner at a high rate of speed barely missing a parked car. I could see that there were at least two images in the fast moving SUV. As the truck sped by me the light in front of it changed to red but the driver continued through the red light barely missing another car that had pulled out who had the green light.

Standing on the steps of my building and looking in the direction of the parking garage I heard the woman cry out John, John, oh God, someone help me, my husband has been shot. Now it was clear to me what I heard so my heart began beating faster and I could feel this tightness in my chest. I asked myself, why would someone shoot, or worse, murder someone in this neighborhood. I reached for my phone and dialed 911 when suddenly I could hear the sounds of sirens in the distance. A 911 operator answered the phone asking what is your emergency? I told the operator that I believe someone had been shot inside a parking garage near my apartment building. The operator asked for my name and address but I only gave her the name of my street and hung-up. Someone else must of heard the shots and the screams and called 911 because shortly after I hung up my phone I could see the police, EMTs, and fire trucks in the distance coming in the direction of the garage.

I took out the keys to the front door of the building that I lived in but decided to wait on the steps of the building hoping to get a glimpse and a better understanding of what just happened. The police cars, EMTs, and fire trucks were now in front of the parking garage. I could still hear loud crying and sobbing coming from the direction of the parking garage. Several police officers entered the garage with their guns drawn. Shortly after entering the garage one officer exited the garage holding the arm of a woman who had blood stains on her hands and clothing crying and repeating out loud, "John, oh John, they shot my John, please help him she repeated, don't let him die". One of the officers yelled to the EMT's that their assistance was needed in the garage.

I stood on my steps nervously thinking to myself, who was John, and why did someone want him dead. I asked myself was this a robbery gone wrong or was the person who was shot an intentional target. And if this was a hit on someone, of all places how could this be happening across the street from my apartment. And how could this be happening in such an affluent neighborhood where some well-known politicians and prominent judges lived.

As I stood on the steps of my building I felt like I was in a plot from a murder mystery and I started feeling like I was slipping into a dark foggy dream that would eventually turn into a nightmare. Even though I knew I was not sleeping, I felt like I was slipping in to a hypnotic state and needed to shake myself and break free of this trance before I got to a point of no return. I had been transfixed for a moment but somehow I had to snap out of this potential nightmare and get inside.

Just as I turned to put my keys in the door I heard a voice say sir, can I speak to you for a moment? I felt this lump in my throat and my hand could not get the key in the door because of how much it was shaking. As I turned in the direction of the voice I saw the uniform first, the gun hanging on his waist, and then the badge. Accompanying the uniform officer was a second man who was wearing a dark gray suit. I turned around and asked the officer how could I help him? The officer in the uniform asked me did I live here? I responded, yes. The gentleman in the suit stated that he was Detective Harrison and that he was investigating a shooting that just occurred in the garage across the street.

I began thinking to myself that I could have been in the wrong place at the wrong time and could have been a victim also. Detective Harrison pulled out a small note pad and a pen and wanted to know what I had seen or heard? I answered that I didn't see or hear anything. Detective Harrison asked where was I coming from and how long have I been standing here. I answered that I am a student at New York University, and a Journalist with The Manhattan Times, and that I just left the library. He stated that you didn't answer my question, once again, how long have you been standing here? I answered that I just arrived home.

The officer in the blue uniform turned around and started walking back toward the garage. Detective Harrison asked me if I drove home or did I walk home from the subway station three blocks away? Because the parking garage is in the pathway between my apartment and the subway station, I confessed that I walked from the subway station to my apartment and that after I had passed the garage I heard sounds that I thought were fireworks. Detective Harrison asked, what else did I hear or see. I asked him if he could tell me more about what just happened before I answer any more questions. The detective answered that the Honorable Judge John Barrows had been shot. I asked the Detective, how is he doing? Detective Harrison stated that he could not answer that question at this time and all he needed now was my name and what I saw and heard. I responded that after I heard the popping sounds I turned around and saw the shadow of a man and heard the footsteps of someone running from the parking garage. After the shadow and the footsteps, I heard the screams of a woman coming from the parking garage.

When I was almost in front of my building I saw a dark colored SUV with two people in it driving at a high rate of speed. I told Detective Harrison that the SUV came from around the corner and ran a red light almost colliding with another vehicle. Detective Harrison asked, what else did you see? I responded, nothing else, that's all I heard or saw, can I go now? The officer responded, not so fast, and why are you so nervous? I responded that I had never witnessed someone being shot before. The officer stated, you just told me you didn't see anything, are you sure there isn't anything else you want to tell me. I responded that what I meant was that I have never been this close to an area where someone had been shot.

I told the detective that I had given him all the information I had and I needed to get up early and I would like to go inside. Detective Harrison gave me one of his cards and asked me for my name and number in the event he ever needed to get in touch with me with additional questions. I gave the Detective my name and number, took his business card, and then went inside.

That evening as I sat on my sofa, I couldn't get the sound of those screams out of my head. Also the image of the woman with blood all over her hands and clothing was an image I couldn't seem to erase. I knew in advance that tonight I could look forward to a sleepless night. I kept thinking over and over in my mind, why would someone shoot a judge, and more specific, Judge Barrows.

That evening I watch several news cast on television hoping to get some information that would help me understand what and why this happened. Finally, as I watched the last newscast for the evening at eleven o'clock the news reporter stated that the Honorable Judge John Barrows, of the Fifth District Court of Appeals, was pronounced dead at approximately ten nineteen, and that he was shot twice in the chest from close range and lived about three hours before succumbing to his wounds. The reporter stated that

Judge Barrows leaved behind to mourn his death, his wife of twenty-nine years, and a son, William, twenty-four years old, and a daughter, Susan, who is twenty-one years old. The reporter stated that Judge Barrows was fifty-one years old and had served on the bench as a judge for seventeen years.

I stayed awake most of the night and managed to get about an hour of sleep before my alarm went off at 6am. That morning as I got dressed I couldn't stop thinking about what happened last night so I left my apartment that morning without breakfast because I had no appetite.

As I passed the garage where the shooting took place I crossed over to the other side of the street because I could not help but think that this could happen again. I could see the police tape around the entrance to the garage and several officers doing investigative work and several news trucks on the scene.

I continued my three block journey to the subway station and upon arriving notice that the newsstand was buzzing with activity. When I asked Jimmy, who was the newsstand owner, what all the activity was about, he said that newspapers were selling like hotcakes and that the shooting last night in our neighborhood was on the front page. I did my best to block the sound of gunfire and screams replaying in my mind, yet I knew that the newspaper article would prompt my mind to relive this nightmare all over again.

Before entering the subway-station I reluctantly picked up a copy of the newspaper to read on the way into work. There was a picture of the garage in the background and I could see the entrance to my apartment building. As I started to feel the moving and jerking of the train I kept asking myself, why would someone murder a prominent New York judge, and whether this was a robbery gone bad or an actual hit. And if this was a hit, what did he do and who did he do it to that they would have the audacity to shoot a judge.

Choices We Make

I was in my final semester as a graduate student studying journalism at New York University. I also work part-time as an investigative reporter for the Manhattan Times that was located in the financial district near Madison Avenue, which was in the heart of the city. A part of me wanted to get this horrific incident out of my mind and emotions, yet the journalist in me was curious and wanted to know more about the who, what, when, where, why and how. If the shooting was a hit, who ordered it and who carried it out. And what did Judge Barrows do to them to make them resort to murder, and what was going to happen next.

I hesitated to open the newspaper on my lap but curiosity overpowered me and when I opened it to the first page there were numerous photos of the neighborhood where the shooting took place. As the train pulled out of 89th Street & Amsterdam Avenue station, I noticed that most of the commuters on the train were doing the same thing I was doing. Everyone was reading the newspaper and those sitting next to me were tuned in to the story about the shooting. Something inside of me led me to believe that everyone else who was reading the newspaper were reading the same story.

It was morning rush hour and the train was full to capacity and the train ride to my job would take about thirty-five minutes. I have been working in the investigation department named Insight as a reporter for the past five years. My hope and desire is to one day win a Pulitzer Prize for writing a fact based amazing story about someone doing a good and kind deed or uncovering a sinister act. I was anxious to get to work so that I could share a firsthand account of what I had witness regarding the shooting of Judge Barrows with my coworkers and find out what they knew. A couple of my coworkers also lived in the city and one lived in the same neighborhood as I did.

Jerry Hanson is the office manager who commutes from the suburb. Tom Webber is the assistant manager who was always the first to arrive at work and the last to leave. He would always make sure that the rest of us was fully aware of his commitment. Lisa Combs, who thought she was God's gift to men, was the accounting manager. Lisa is fifty-three going on seventeen, and she dresses the part. Susan Mitchell is my supervisor who lives about eight blocks from me but never once offered me a ride to or from work. She lives with her female partner and made sure that the men in our department and other departments knew where she stood. And finally there is Stan Jenkins who lives in Greenwich Village with his partner Mike who works upstairs in distribution. Mike makes it his business to visit our office at least twice a day to check up on Stan to make sure he is behaving himself, if you know what I mean. Even though the Manhattan Times has almost four thousand employees I only know and associate with those in my immediate department.

When I arrived at work I inquired with my coworkers about their knowledge of the shooting of Judge Barrows on the upper west side of Manhattan that was the hot topic of the morning. Because of the high profile nature of the story it was being covered by at least three departments that were going to offer different perspectives of the story. The three departments at the newspaper that would be covering the story from different angles were, the political, the business, and my department, the investigative, which was called Insight. Because I was new to the investigation department compared to Stan or Tom I knew that it was unlikely that I would be assigned to cover the story. It was obvious by the unusual number of visits to both Stan and Tom office by Jerry that both of them really wanted to be assigned the lead to cover the story.

Later that morning Jerry scheduled an office meeting to discuss the latest events surrounding the shooting of the Judge Barrows and to assign the story to a reporter. I could tell by the tension in the air and the expression on Jerry's face that this was a tough decision to make because both senior reporters wanted the story. After doing a lousy job of trying to appease Stan, Jerry announced that Tom would be covering the story and he wanted everyone to be supportive and assist Tom in any way we could. Tom made a comment that he wanted to have a department meeting once a week to share current information and stay abreast of the latest developments surrounding the shooting. The shooting of a prominent judge was no small matter and every reporter knew that an opportunity to cover a story of this magnitude was the diamond in the ruff.

It was a Thursday evening in the month of September that Judge Barrows was shot to death by an unknown assailant and we the Manhattan Times or the New York Police department had no clue as to a motive. Friday had come and gone and we had made decisions about who and how the story would be covered. During the weekend I tried my best to focus on my personal life and get back to my routines nevertheless I couldn't shake the feeling that the shooting meant more than meets the eye.

It was Sunday morning and I decided that I would go for a walk hoping it would help me to relax and take my mind off the events of the past few days. It was a quiet morning in the neighborhood and the leaves were letting the world know that fall was in the air. I had finished my walk and was about to return to my apartment when the thought entered my mind to walk over to the underground garage where the shooting took place. I stood in front of the garage and could see inside where the police tape was still near the exact spot where the shooting took place. The garage had been closed since the shooting and was scheduled to reopen on Wednesday. I was a few feet from the chalk outline of where the body of Judge Barrows had laid. I was hesitant at first but decided to walk over to the outline to get a closer look. As I moved closer to the outline I began to see the shooting play out in my imagination. It was a strange feeling to stand over the area where someone was murdered. As I looked closer on the ground where the outline was I noticed a coin about the size of a dime. I picked up the coin to examine it closer and realize that it was not real but a gold colored hard plastic coin with two capital A's on one side and a dove on the opposite side.

Symbols Of Justice

There was something strange and unusual about the coin and how it was place near the outline of the body. It was placed in the center of the head area of the body's outline. I put the coin in my pocket and decided to return to my apartment. As I sat in my apartment staring at the coin in my hand a thousand thoughts ran through my mind. Somehow I knew in my heart of hearts that this coin told a story about the shooting and the motive for the shooting. There could be only one of two reasons why the coin was where I found it. Either someone drop the coin accidentally while walking by or the shooter returned to the crime scene and intentionally placed the coin on the outline of the body. I had spent the rest of the day thinking about the coin and watching television from time to time.

It was about six o'clock in the evening and I make it my business not to miss the evening news. A news flash came across the screen stating that there was a shooting in Lower Manhattan and as soon as they get more information they would make it available. I could tell by the broadcast, the number of policemen, firemen, and other first responders on the scene that this involved someone of importance. It was near the end of the broadcast when the newscaster finally released the name of the person that was injured in the attack. He stated that city Councilman Harry Ford was shot twice while jogging near his home and he was rushed to Manhattan General Hospital. The newscaster went on to say that they had no current information about the councilman's condition but as soon as they know more they would share it with the public.

The past few days left me bewildered trying to wrap my head around what happened to Judge Barrows and now Councilman Harry Ford. I decided to turn in early to hopefully get a good night rest knowing that work tomorrow would be challenging and possibly overwhelming because of recent events.

As I walked into the office Monday morning I could sense by the atmosphere that something unusual and newsworthy had happened. I was running a few minutes late so as I approach the conference room where we held our morning meetings I felt the stare of all eyes on me. Jerry looked at his watch and then looked up at me shaking his head stating that I would be late for my own wedding. Everyone in the room chuckled as I sat at the table and apologized for my tardiness.

Jerry began the meeting by sharing that for those who may not already know, Councilman Harry Ford was shot twice last night and succumbed to his wounds at Manhattan General Hospital. He died at 11:40pm while undergoing surgery. Jerry went on to say that Councilman Ford was fifty-three years old and left behind to mourn his passing was his wife of twenty-five years and three teenage children. He also stated that currently the police department had not arrested anyone and had no suspects or witnesses or motive for the shooting.

Jerry shared that the police department reported that they did find and unusual object at the scene of the shooting that they believe was intentionally left by someone. They were not sure if it was related to the shooting and at this time they were not releasing details about the description of the object that was found. I thought about the coin that I had found yesterday while I was out walking and whether what the police found was similar or the same. I left the coin home in one of my dresser drawers and decided that I would not reveal this information at this time with my coworkers.

Jerry decided to assign the story about Councilman Ford's shooting to Stan and stated that since I was the junior reporter and had never covered a major story before that I would be assisting both Tom and Stan with investigating the shootings.

I have had the opportunity to work with Stan in the past but I have never had the opportunity to work closely with Tom. Working with Stan in the past had always been a pleasant and rewarding experience but there were rumors throughout the office and other departments that working with Tom was like pulling teeth from a rattlesnake and that he was rude and condescending. Knowing this I wanted to go to Jerry and create a fictitious story telling him why it would be better to find someone else to work with Tom. On the other hand, I knew that in order to get an opportunity to be assigned a major story I would have to take the good with the bad. I informed both Tom and Stan that I would make some calls to my contacts that I had in the community and report to them later as to what information I uncovered about the shootings. I also knew that the best and most reliable information I could uncover would come from face to face conversations and dispensing the green motivator.

I grew up in the mid-west and had moved to New York five years ago to pursue my education and a career as a journalist. My father wanted me to follow in his footsteps and become a doctor. My mother on the other hand who was a school teacher was okay with me finding my own way as long as what I did provided enough income so I could live on my own and help others. I had two siblings, an older brother Robert, who joined the military so that they would eventually pay for his education so he could become a doctor. And a younger sister Karen, who had an adventurous spirit, and after two years dropped out of college to join a rock band.

My contacts in the community were people most would describe as unscrupulous characters, nevertheless they knew the ins and outs of the neighborhood and who was doing what, when and

The Anointed Assassin

why. The information that I obtained from these contacts had to be handled with discretion and be verified carefully before going to press and released to the public. One of the things that all of my contacts had in common was that none of them would use their real name. All of them would use what is known as a handle, which is similar to a nickname.

The first call I made was to a contact who use the handle Streetwise. Streetwise was a twenty-three years old unemployed Italian kid who lives with his girlfriend who is employed as 911 operator for the New York City Police Department. Little did she know that her live in boyfriend was manipulating and using her for information about events and crimes that he would later sell to the highest bidder.

I dialed Streetwise number and as usual he answered on the first ring. He was always excited about hearing from me because he knew that he could look forward to being compensated with the green motivator. I knew that Streetwise had been a reliable source of information for news stories that I had written in the past and hopefully he would come through with this new story. And because of some known bad habits and character flaws that he displayed I had to be cautious about the information he provided. And as the saying goes, take it with a grain of salt. In other words, I had to verify and cross check his information with other sources and other contacts.

I asked Streetwise did he hear about the shootings that happen to two prominent people in the city over the past few days. I intentionally chose not to give names because I knew that by doing so I would be giving him ammunition to create a bogus story just to collect the green motivator. One of the things a good journalist is taught is to not give your source to much information in the pursuit of inside information. There had been countless shootings in the city over the past week and I was only looking for information about two of them. Based on my question about the shooting of two prominent people I waited for his answer.

It was music to my ear when Streetwise spoke in the phone, are you referring to the shootings of Judge John Barrows and Councilman Harry Ford. I responded yes, what have you heard on the streets and is there any information that you have that could be helpful with solving the murders. I already knew what he was going to say next. He answered that he had heard a few things but his memory was a little foggy. That was Streetwise way of sayings, if you have the green motivator, a.k.a., dead presidents, a.k.a., money, his memory would clear up and return. I had learned from past experience not to discuss the specifics of a story with a source over the phone. I asked Streetwise was he available to meet me at the usual place on

The Anointed Assassin

Eighth Ave around three o'clock. He agreed to the time and place and reminded me to stop by the ATM machine.

One of the risk you take as an investigative journalist when relying on paid sources for information is accuracy, authenticity, and truth. Nothing is more embarrassing and has the potential for a lawsuit is when you print a story that is not based on truth and facts and is potentially slanderous. Whatever information I would obtain from Streetwise later today I would have to verify and cross-check it with my other sources. One of the perks or benefit that came with my position with the newspaper is that you are given an allowance to help cover the cost of using sources to get the goods, the dirt, the facts, etc., that is used to write headlines stories. I caught a taxi and arrived at the location where I was meeting Streetwise about fifteen minutes early. When I went inside and looked around I could see Streetwise sitting in the back of the cafe with his hat almost pulled down over his face as if he was trying to disguise himself. Because it was around three O'clock in the afternoon and Monday the Cafe had only a few patrons. I sat down at the table and greeted Streetwise. He nodded back and ask did I make the stop that we discussed. I told Streetwise he needed to slow his roll and to let's take one thing at a time.

I informed Streetwise that he looked a few

pounds lighter since the last time we met a few months earlier. I asked jokingly, is everything alright, are you on a diet. In the back of my mind I had a pretty good idea what caused the fluctuation in Streetwise weight. Streetwise lived and survived by his savvy and wits and depended on his street credibility to get inside information. Along the way he had picked up some illegal and expensive habits that affected him physically and financially.

I asked Streetwise what information did he have for me about what happened to the Judge and the Councilman? He responded that depended on what I had for him. I told Streetwise that I have what we discussed on the phone. I asked Streetwise to tell me what he knew or have heard about the shootings of Judge Barrows and Councilman Ford? I told him if I like what I hear and I can verify it I would give him a hundred dollars now and another hundred after his information is confirmed. And if I didn't like what I hear I would give him fifty dollars for wasting both of our time.

Streetwise stated that the word on the street is that there is a group who has vowed to clean up the city by getting rid of corrupt individuals who call themselves public servants. I asked Streetwise what is the name of the group and how many members are there in the group and how are they funded. He replied that he didn't know the name of group but heard that there were about twenty-five members and growing. I ask him how do they recruit members and where do they meet? Streetwise replied that he didn't know but if I gave him a hundred for the current information and extra hundred in advance he would find out within two days. I asked Streetwise did he think the information he had given me so far was worth a hundred dollars. He responded that the information was solid and that I could take it to the bank. I told Streetwise that I needed more specifics for this information to be worth anything that I can use to print a story. I asked him was there a way that I could verify that his information was authentic and a way to confirm it.

Streetwise began to get antsy in his seat and stated sharply he needed to be somewhere and that he did his part and delivered good information and wanted to get paid. I gave Streetwise one of my cards and a hundred dollars and told him if I can verify what he told me and he could get me the name of the group and the name of the leaders I would give him another hundred dollars, maybe more. He took the hundred dollars from my hand quickly and said okay, okay.

I returned to the office and sat at my desk thinking about the information Streetwise shared with me and whether I was being sent on a wild goose chase. It was now after four O'clock so I decided to call it a day and head home. I knew that the next few days would be spent confirming what

I had been told using my other sources. A part of me wanted and hoped the information was true but in my gut I had feelings of doubt.

The following day as I headed in to work around noon I decided stop by Barney's, a twenty-four-hour bar, to see one of my other contacts. I walked in the bar and could hardly see or breathe because of the smoke and the smell. I looked around the bar a few minutes before asking the bartender if he had seen Cosmos and if he had been in the bar recently. He responded that Cosmos was in the bar a few days ago and when he comes in again he would inform him that I was looking for him. I gave the bartender one of my cards to pass on to Cosmos and thanked him and headed in to the office.

Who, What, When, Where, and Why

As I walked into the office I was anxious to know what my coworkers had uncovered about the shootings of Judge Barrows and Councilman Ford. About an hour after I arrived at work that morning Jerry scheduled a meeting to discuss the latest developments related to the shootings. During the meeting Jerry asked each of us if there was information we wanted to share that could help the senior writers, Tom and Stan, develop their stories. There was an uncomfortable silence in the room for a minute before Jerry remind us that this was an important and crucial story that the newspaper needed to get the jump on it before other media groups beat us to it. After clearing my throat, I stated that I had made contact with one of my sources who had given me some information that I needed to confirm. I added that if and when I am able to confirm the sources information it may give some insight into why both shootings took place.

Jerry ask me if I could elaborate and share some specifics about the information and the source. I responded that I would prefer waiting until I could verify and confirm the information with a second or possibly third source before I pass it on. Tom asserted with a snarling and sharp tone, that if I had any information that could assist with putting together a front page story that I need to share it and not sit on it. He went on to say that if I ever wanted to become a professional journalist that I had to be more forthcoming and supportive of senior reporters. Immediately I looked over at Stan and Jerry to see if they agreed with Tom and shared his attitude. I could see by their facial expressions that both were not in agreement and finally Stan spoke and said we should wait until the information was verified with my other sources.

Jerry commented that we shouldn't get ahead of ourselves and reminded everyone that we were on the same team. Jerry asked me to do him and the newspaper a big favor and to focus on my contacts related to the shootings and to put any other assignments I had on the shelf until after the story about the shootings is printed.

After the meeting I returned to my office with mixed emotions concerning Tom's comment about sharing information with senior reporters and becoming a professional journalist. On the other hand, I remembered the rumors in the various departments concerning how difficult it can be working with Tom.

I decided to check my voice mail to see if I had a message from Cosmos or Streetwise with additional information related to the shootings. I was overjoyed and excited when I heard the message from Cosmos saying he had some important information related to the shootings of Judge Barrows and Councilman Ford. I immediately dialed the contact number Cosmos left on my voicemail to reach him. The voice on the other end of the phone was not Cosmos. It was a female voice who sounded like she was under the influence of something.

I asked her was Cosmos available? She asked with a slurring voice, who was this calling, how did I know Cosmos, and what did I want with him? I told her my name and that I was a journalist with the Manhattan Times and that Cosmos had work with me in the past on important stories. She said that she was his fiancé and that he had mentioned it to her that I might be calling. She went on to say that he wasn't there and that as soon as he returned she would give him the message that I called. I thanked her and asked what her name was? She stated that she would prefer not to share her name but assured me that he would get the message that I called and the next thing I heard was a dial tone. I thought to myself WOW, was it something I said. It was about noon time so I decided to take a lunch break which for me was a yogurt, a banana, and a fifteen-minute nap with my head on my desk. Shortly after I laid my head on my desk my phone rang. I sat up straight, stretched quickly, and answered, Insight department, Terry Carter speaking. The voice on the phone said this is Cosmos. I asked Cosmos how he was and told him that I stopped by Barney's Pub looking for him earlier today. I informed Cosmos that I heard his voicemail message stating that he had some important information for me. He responded that he heard through the grapevine that I was looking for information about the shootings of a couple of important public officials. I answered yes, what do you have for me and when can we meet? He responded that he heard a few things from reliable sources and wanted to meet later this afternoon around 3:30pm at Barney's Pub. I stated that I would be there 3:30pm sharp and reminded him if he had something of value I would make it well worth his time. I hung up the phone excited about the possibility of getting information to either corroborate or disprove the information I had gotten from Streetwise.

Whichever way it went at least I would know if I was on the right track. Barney's Pub was only about fifteen minutes away from the office so I decided to do some housekeeping for the next two hours before leaving to meet Cosmos.

As I walked out the front door on to the busy New York street I was blinded by the light of the sun shining directly in my eyes. I shielded my eyes with my hand while reaching in my jacket pocket for my sun glasses. It was a warm and bright sunny afternoon in Manhattan and the street was packed with people, vendors, cars, buses and taxis. It took me less than a minute to hail down a cab and within a matter of minutes we were in front of the pub.

I was looking forward to seeing and talking with Cosmos about the shooting but not the smoke and the smell I would have to endure at Barney's Pub. As soon as I entered the pub my eyes and nose started burning. The first person that I made eye contact with was the bartender that I left the card with a few days earlier.

Because this wasn't my first time meeting Cosmos here I knew he would be near the back corner facing the door. For some reason most if not all of the contacts I have ever dealt with would sit in the back of the bar or pub facing the door. All of them said they felt safer with their back to the wall facing the door.

As I got closer to the table where Cosmos was sitting his eyes lit up as he stood to greet me. I reached out my hand to Cosmos as he was reaching his towards me announcing that he had some great news for me. I responded great, that is the kind of business I'm into, the news business.

I asked Cosmos what could he tell me about the shootings of Judge Barrows and Councilman Ford? He stated that the word on the street is that both men were targeted by a group of skinheads who serve time for one reason or the other and has vowed to get revenge by taking out those who are a part a corrupt system. Cosmos stated that he also heard from a reliable source that they are not finish and there will be more of the same in the future. I asked Cosmos on a scale of one to ten how reliable is his source and did he know the name of the group? Cosmos said that if he is not mistaken the name he was given was The Sons of Anarchy. I asked Cosmos who was the group leaders, the location of their headquarters, and how may members were currently in the group? He answered that he didn't have the name of the leaders but he was told the group currently had about fifty members throughout the five boroughs of New York City.

Cosmos stated that there were three unique features about members of the group, first, all of them have serve time in prison, second, all the members have ball heads, and third, all the members have a skull tattoo on their forearm. I told Cosmos that the information seemed to show a plausible motive for the shootings but I still needed to verify it for authenticity. I told him that I needed contact information for the group because I would like to interview the leaders and do a feature story on the group's mission and objectives.

I asked Cosmos did he know what the groups plans were for the near future and whether they were looking at any specific targets or individuals? Cosmos responded that he was confident that he could secure that information but he would need to be compensated handsomely because it would involve him taking a dangerous risk. I asked Cosmos how much did I owe him for the information he just shared? Cosmos responded that the usual amount would cover it but the new information I wanted would be twice as much, maybe more. I asked Cosmos did he mean a hundred dollars? He looked at me with a grimace on his face and whispered, you are kidding me right. Cosmos stated that the usual amount is two hundred dollars but he was thinking that the information was worth a lot more. I decided not to argue with him so I slipped him

The Anointed Assassin

the two hundred dollars on the down low and told him that it would be nice to hear from him within the next two days.

As I left the Pub I could feel my eyes burning from the cigarette and cigar smoke that was everywhere. It was almost five o'clock and the work day was coming to a close so rather than going back to the office I decided to call it day and head home. The thought came to my mind that the information Streetwise shared with me and the information Cosmos shared with me had some similarities but I would need more information before knowing for sure. The big mystery was, were they describing the same group or a two different group, or could both group be a figment of their imagination. My hope was that both group described was actually the same group and one of my sources would provide me contact information for the group leaders that would help me identify the group responsible for the assassinations.

The following day on my way to work I pondered the reason for the plastic coin that I found at the murder scene that had two capital A in the center of a circle and a dove on the opposite side. In addition to that I thought about the detective who investigated the second murder reporting that a strange object was found at the scene and their reason for not wanting to disclose details or share the description of the item at this time. Of course I could not help but wonder if the object found at the location of Councilman Ford's murder was similar or exactly like what I had found at the location where Judge Barrows was murdered. I decided that rather than let curiosity eat me alive I would visit the police precinct that was handling Councilman Ford's murder case and speak with the lead detective.

The Good, The Bad, And Law Enforcement

After doing some research I found out that the Fourth Precinct was handling the case and that the lead detective on the case was Detective Harry Smith. I asked myself which would be the best approach, just showing up unannounced or calling the precinct hoping to get Detective Smith on the phone and make an appointment to meet with him. I decided I would call first and hope for the best. In the past trying to go this route to get information had failed miserably. I dialed the number to the precinct and after at least ten rings finally a voice answers, Fourth Precinct, how may I direct your call. I responded, Detective Harry Smith please. I was transferred to Detective Smith extension but got his voice mail. I waited and hour and the same thing happen. After five attempts I knew what I had to do.

The Fourth Precinct was located in Lower Manhattan around 34th Street, about a twenty-minute ride by taxi from my office. As I sat in the back of the taxi I tried formulating in my mind the questions that I would ask the detective to uncover information about the object that was found at the murder scene of Councilman Ford. My hope was to get the information from Detective Smith without letting him know about the coin I found at the location where Judge Barrows was murdered.

The traffic was heavy so it gave me extra time to map out my thoughts and construct my line of questioning. As I arrived at the precinct it seemed I had walked into a sea of blue. There were uniform police officers everywhere as well as a few detectives dressed in cheap gray and blue suits and wearing high shine Oxford shoes. I could also tell by the way they were dressed that some of them were well disguise undercover officers.

I felt a little intimidated at first but mustered up the courage and walked up the steps to the front door. When I open the door to go in two of the officers walked right through as if I opened the door for them, bumping in to me neither saying thank you or excuse me. I said to myself that I hope this is not what I can expect from the rest of my visit.

As I approach the front desk I could see from the insignia on his arm that the big burly gentleman behind the desk was a sergeant. I thought to myself that maybe some of the preconceive notions people held about police officers may be true because the Sergeant behind the desk was holding a donut in one hand and a cup of coffee in the other as he asked me, can I help you? I responded that I was a reporter with the Manhattan Times and that I wanted to speak with Detective Smith. The sergeant stuffed a piece of donut in his mouth and asked me, who did you say you were? There was a lot of background noise from the heavy traffic of people in the lobby of the station so I blamed the surroundings and not the donut for his inability to hear and understand what I said. I repeated myself to the sergeant but this time louder leaning over the desk towards him. He responded, well you don't have to yell, stating that his hearing works just fine. He pointed to a hallway and said that Detective Harris office was the third door on the right but he didn't think that Detective Harris was in, but I was free to go look for myself. I thanked the sergeant and walked down the hall hoping he was wrong and Detective Harris would be in his office waiting and happy to see me.

Unfortunately, Sergeant Friday was right, Detective Harris was not there. I decided to leave my card in his mailbox outside of his office with a note on the back about why I was here. I must admit that I was a bit frustrated by not being able to connect with Detective Harris and also the attitude of the front desk sergeant.

It was about three o'clock and since I had no pressing or urgent work concerns I decided I would camp out in the lobby and wait for Detective Harris. After waiting about ninety minutes and approaching five different detectives, finally the sixth was Detective Harris. After introducing myself and telling him that I am a reporter for the Manhattan Times working on a story about the murders of Judge Barrows and Councilman Ford, Detective Harris invited me to his office.

Detective Harris offered me a seat and ask me how could he be of assistance? I asked Detective Harris has the investigation turned up any suspects or uncovered any motives for the shootings? He stated that as of yet there are no suspects and they have no information about why the shootings took place. I said to Detective Harris that I understand that there was an unusual object found at the scene of the shooting of Councilman Ford and could he elaborate and give a description of the object that was found. He responded that unfortunately because it was early in the investigation that he would not be able to disclose any details about the object that was found but stated that the object could fit in your pocket. Detective Harris stated that it seemed as if the object was left there purposely to possibly make a statement. He went on to say that if the object was in fact left to make a statement, they currently have no idea what message they were trying to send.

I informed Detective Harris that I would like to contact him from time to time in the future to follow up on the latest information uncovered in the investigation. He agreed and stated that the information he could share may be limited if it could compromise the investigation. Detective Harris and I exchange business cards and after thanking him I left the police station thinking about the object that they found that could fit in your pocket and the coin I found and whether there was a connection.

That evening while at home doing some research on the shootings and watching the news a report came over the air about another shooting. The reporter stated that state representative Sam Harden was gunned down while coming out of restaurant near his home around 5:30pm. The reporter stated that he was with his wife of 31 years and that he was pronounced dead at the scene of the shooting. Witnesses at the scene of the shooting stated that a lone gunman wearing a mass committed the crime and ran from the scene immediately. The reporter went on to say that a bystander noticed that the shooter reached down and placed an object near the representative's head which later was described as a plastic coin resembling the description of the coin that I found. The reporter stated that Representative Harden had one son who was currently away studying at Atlanta University.

It had been a few days since I spoke with my contacts Streetwise and Cosmos and I wondered if they may of uncovered any more information and details about who or what group was behind the shootings. I thought about calling them even though it was late evening but decided to wait until the morning to reach out to them.

All three men was killed in Manhattan. Judge Barrows case was being investigated by the third precinct, Councilman Ford by the fourth precinct, and State Representative Harden by the 2nd precinct. Because the investigation was currently being handled by three different detectives this would make it challenging to communicate with them to find out if they were on the same page in determining a connection.

Talk to Me

The next morning shortly after arriving at work Jerry announce an office meeting to see where everyone was at with information about the shootings. He started the meeting with news about the latest shooting of State Representative Harden which we all were already aware of. He asked the team what new developments did any of us have related to the events of the past week. Everyone stated that there weren't any new developments or anything of significance they could offer. I shared that two of my contacts provided information about two groups and their motives for the shootings that had similarities.

I asked my coworkers were they aware of reports that at the shootings of Councilman Ford and Representative Harden that an object was left at the scene, possibly by the shooter. Everyone in the group responded that they were aware that something was left but had no detail information about the description of the object. I informed the group that I would be reaching out to my contacts later today to see if they had any additional information, details, or specifics about who is responsible for the shootings.

After the morning meeting I went to my office to start making calls to my contacts Cosmos and Streetwise. I had a few more contacts that I occasionally use but these two were my main sources for information related to violent street level offenses. I decided that I would call Streetwise first because his information had more details than Cosmos and I had a gut feeling there was some truth to his information. I dialed Streetwise number and after ringing a few times he answered the phone, Wise, who's this? I answered that this was Terry Carter. With excitement in his voice, he responded, Terry, what's up man. I stated that I was calling to see if he came across any additional information related to who is responsible for the shootings. He responded that he wasn't feeling well and that he had a lead on some information but was too sick to follow up on it. He asked me would I be willing to give him an advance on the information that he was going to secure and guaranteed me that it was a solid lead.

When Streetwise said he was sick I knew he wasn't referring to being sick in the traditional way most of us think of being sick. I hesitated before saying to Streetwise that I wasn't comfortable with this arrangement but I would make an exception this one time. I told Streetwise to meet me at the usual place around noon and I would give him an advance of fifty dollars.

My next call was to Cosmos who answered the phone on the first ring. I ask Cosmos did he have any additional information related to the shootings? He stated that he did have some basic information but no details that was significant and he would call me when he did have something meaningful or noteworthy.

That afternoon after meeting with Streetwise and giving him the advance I decided to visit the three murder scenes to see if I could find something the investigating detectives may have overlooked. I took some pictures at each of the location where the murders were committed but after closely examining the pictures there wasn't anything that stood out at any of the location. Even though I hadn't seen it with my own eyes I knew in my heart of hearts that the strange object that was found at the second crime scene was the same as the coin that was found at the first and third crime scenes.

That evening at home while watching the evening news the reporter stated that they had invited a group who was concern about the recent violence and shootings in the city to speak and make an announcement. The group leaders consisted of a Catholic Priest, a Baptist Minister, a Muslim Imam and a Jewish Rabbi. The religious and spiritual leaders stated on the newscast that they were putting aside their difference because they believed that only by working together they could make a bigger impact and bring about positive changes in the community, the city, and the world.

I almost fell of my sofa as I watched the television screen and heard that these four faith leaders with such strong difference in doctrine and beliefs was willing to work together. I thought to myself that this collaboration would probably last less than a week. The newscaster went on to say that the four leaders would be holding their first community meeting on Tuesday night at 7pm at the YMCA on 8th Avenue and 125th Street to discuss how they can work together with local residents to stop the violence aa well as solve other community problems. Everyone from the five boroughs were invited to come

The Anointed Assassin

and share and be a part of the meeting and to help make a difference in their neighborhoods.

I decided that I would attend this meeting to see and hear if there was any information I could obtain about the shootings and to see if I could meet new contacts like Streetwise and Cosmos. That evening at the meeting there were about a hundred and fifty residents representing the five boroughs.

A Meeting Of The Minds

The first person to speak was the Baptist preacher, Pastor John Hammond from the Eighth Avenue Baptist Church. He stated to the audience the purpose for the meeting and why the four faith leaders had joined forces in hopes of getting their congregations to work with individuals of different faith, cultures and perspectives. He went on to say that the four faith leaders would be working on a name for the group and a mission statement and that the group would meet the first Tuesday of every month at this location at 7pm. He stated that each of the leaders would come to the podium and introduce themselves and then there would be an open discussion. The Baptist preacher ended by saying "may God bless and protect all of you and your families.

The next to approach the podium was the Muslim Imam, who introduced himself as Imam Amir Abdullah, who stated he represented the Hubun Mosque that is located on 125th Street and Saint Nicholas Avenue. He spoke in Arabic, "As-Salaam-Alaykum", which means, "Peace Be Upon You".

The next to introduce himself was a Jewish Rabbi, who introduce himself as Rabbi Abraham Belenky, and stated he was the Rabbi of Temple Sinai, located on the corner of Central and Jefferson Avenues. He stated all were welcome and he would pray that everyone would be blessed and protected from the violence taking over our city.

The last leader to approach the podium was the Catholic Priest, who introduce himself as Father Nicholas Gage, who stated that he presided over St. Joseph Catholic Church, located at the corner of Seneca and Dekalb Avenues. He stated that to his knowledge this is the first time a group this diverse in faith has come together to make an attempt to address the violence and other issues in our neighborhoods. Father Gage added that he hoped that everyone present would continue to come to the meetings and tell their neighbors and friends. He said a prayer by St. Augustine,"Our hearts are restless Oh Lord, until they rest in You'', then announced that the meeting was open for questions and discussions and then left the podium.

I raised my hand and stood up and stated that my name was Terry Carter and that I was an inves-

The Anointed Assassin

tigative reporter from the Manhattan Times and that I was investigating the shootings of Judge Barrows, Councilman Ford and State Representative Harden. I stated that my question is for the faith leaders that organized the meeting, and the question is, do you currently have any information related to the shootings of these public servants? The four faith leaders looked at each other with a puzzled look on their face and after thirty seconds of silence that was somewhat awkward, Rabbi Belenky answered that to his knowledge none of them had any information about who was responsible for the shootings.

He went on to announce that if anyone in the meeting had any information about these shootings to please inform the police department and/or share it with one of them. The meeting lasted about an hour but nothing of substance that would help my investigation was shared. Finally, Pastor Hammond approach the podium and thanked everyone for coming and reminded them to attend the next meeting the first Tuesday of next month and to tell their friends and neighbors.

The following day at work Tom scheduled a 10am meeting to discuss the latest developments related to the shootings. He opened the meeting by asking who had any information that has not been previously discussed. After a moment of silence, I shared with my coworkers that what I was about to say they may find difficult to believe. I shared that I attended a community meeting last night that was organized by a Rabbi, a Baptist preacher, a Muslim Imam, and a Catholic priest. All of my coworkers gave me a look as if to indicate that I was fabricating this working relationship between the faith leaders. I raised my right hand as a sign that I was being truthful.

Finally, Tom spoke and said Terry, you don't have a great sense of humor but you have a vivid imagination, do you expect us to believe such an incredible and unbelievable tale as that. I responded that I found it hard to believe until I saw it with my own eyes and heard it with my own ears, but it did happen. The faith leaders stated that they were concerned about the increased violence in the city and were willing to put aside their differences in the hopes of bringing about needed positive changes in the city. I informed my coworkers that the next open meeting will be held the first Tuesday of next month if they were interested in attending to witness this phenomenon for themselves.

I could tell by the expression on their faces that this information about the leaders left everyone dazed and at a loss for words. Tom ended the meeting by stating that he wanted me to do a follow up by attending the next meeting and any subsequent meetings they might hold. Tom was about to end the meeting when his secretary

The Anointed Assassin

knocked on the door and stuck her head inside and said turn on the television. Tom turned on the television set in the conference room and there was a news bulletin on the screen.

All Hell Breaks Loose

The newscaster reported that they were bringing important breaking news from the scene of the shooting of Congressman Steve Willis. The reporter stated that Congressman Willis was shot twice in the back while leaving a hotel in the downtown area with an unidentified young woman. The reporter went on to say that currently they had no information regarding the condition of the Congressman and that he was being rush to Saint Mary's Hospital in lower Manhattan. I immediately asked Tom and the others to excuse me because I wanted to go to the scene of the crime to see if the item I found at the location where Judge Barrows was shot would also be found at the location where Congressman Willis was just shot.

As my taxi approached the street where the hotel was located there was bumper to bumper traffic extending about three blocks. After about twenty minutes of sitting in traffic we finally reached the hotel and I could see the yellow crime tape near the side entrance of the hotel. As I walked toward the yellow tape I theorized about the plastic coin I had at home and what the two A's on one side and the dove on the other side meant.

Because it was almost five hours after the shooting the crime scene where the shooting took place was now free of police activity so I felt comfortable snooping around. It took about ten minutes of searching before I saw the gold plastic coin near the curve a few feet from the hotel door. After finding this strange coin at two separate locations where a judge and a politician was killed and a similar coin also found at the location where Representative Harden was murdered, I was confident that the object the police found where Councilman's Ford was murdered was also a coin. It goes without saying that there is a connection between these crimes and the question that has to be answered is who is behind these assassinations and why.

My mind kept racing back and forth between who was committing these murders, why they were committing them and how was I and/or the police going to solve this mystery. I knew that if I was able to unravel this puzzle I could have an exclusive story worthy of a Pulitzer Prize. I knew that I had an uphill battle ahead of me and possibly a dangerous one but I had made up in my mind that I would see this story through to the end.

I decided that maybe it was time to reach

out to my contacts Cosmo and Streetwise, and I also needed to find some new additional ones. It had been about two weeks since I had spoken to either one and I was hoping maybe they would have some new information for me. One location that could be ideal place for meeting new contacts that could provide inside information about who's doing what on the down low and on the streets might be at the monthly community meeting hosted by the faith leaders.

The next community meeting was two weeks away so that evening from home I called both Cosmos and Streetwise to arrange to meet with them. I arranged to meet with Cosmos the next day which was Wednesday but was unable to reach Streetwise. Both Cosmos and Streetwise had given me valuable clues and tips that led to inside information leading to exclusive stories. And on other occasions the tips and information they provided led me down a dead end street. Unfortunately, that was part of the risk you take when you use informants and street level sources for information.

The next day I arrived at the pub around 2:45pm because I've made it a habit to arrive fifteen minutes early when meeting a source. I went inside and sat at the bar near the back so I could watch the door to see when Cosmos arrived. I ordered a club soda to pass the time and once Cosmos arrived then we would move to a booth or table near the back of the bar so that our conversation would be private. As I was sitting there waiting my mind kept imagining all the different scenarios surrounding who might be responsible for these hideous acts of violence and why. A thought would come to my mind asking the question, did these men who were public servants somehow deserve what happened to them? Then another thought would quickly follow asking the question, what could they have done that was so horrible that they deserve a penalty of death?

Finally, about five minutes after three Cosmos walked through the front door of the bar. I waved to him and got up from the bar and walk to a booth in the back of the pub. I greeted Cosmos and as usual he wanted to sit on the side of the booth so that he would be facing the door. I had met Cosmos here at this Pub many times in the past and I was always curious about his reasoning for wanting to sit so he could watch the door. I decided that maybe it was time to ask him the question about why he sat so that he could watch the door. His answer was that in his line of work you can never be too careful and that it was always better to be safe than sorry.

I reminded Cosmos that the last time we spoke that he stated that the group that was responsible for assassinating these public officials was a group called Sons of Anarchy. I asked Cosmos had that information change or is it still the same? Cosmos stated that on the streets the information hasn't change about who is responsible for the shootings. He went on to say that there are some rumors floating around that another unidentified smaller group is responsible. He stated that he would try to get more information about this smaller group but his money was on the Sons of Anarchy. He went on to say that he would also gather more information about the Sons of Anarchy also and keep his eyes and ears open for other possible leads.

Cosmos reminded me that snooping around and digging into groups, cults and street gang backgrounds who commit these kinds of acts can be dangerous. That was Cosmos way of urging me to generous when it came to compensating him for the information he uncovered for me. I gave him a hundred dollars and thanked him for his help nevertheless he held the money with his hand still open. I told him that was the best I could do for the information he just delivered and more would come when he delivered detailed information.

It was now near the end of the day so after leaving Cosmos I decided that I would call it a day. I thought to myself that I could finish the rest of what I needed to get done today working from home. My next task was to get a hold of Streetwise to see what additional information if any that he may have come across. That evening from home around seven O'clock I decide to give Streetwise a call and hopefully arrange to meet him at Barney's tomorrow. I dialed Streetwise number but there was no answer and there was no voice mail or answering machine for me to leave a message. As a journalist you have to accept the reality that when you use informants sometimes the relationship can be short lived.

About an hour later my telephone rang and when I answered it Streetwise was on the other end. I asked him how did he know to return my call since he didn't have voicemail. He stated that he has caller ID on his phone but his answering machine was not working at this time. With a chuckle and in a sarcastic way I responded that in your line of work you need to make sure your answering machine works. I told him thanks for returning my call and that I was hoping we could meet tomorrow around three O'clock at Barney's. He stated that he was looking forward to it and that he had some juicy inside information that was fresh on the streets. I told Streetwise that I was looking forward to seeing him and hearing what he had to share and then we both hung up the phone.

It has been over a month since the first shooting happen near my apartment. I thought about the information Cosmos gave me and wondered whether it was credible or if I was being sent, as they say, on a wild goose chase. I decided to turn in early so that I could get a good night rest.

The next day at work Tom, the assistant

head editor, came by my office to ask if I had any leads or information related to the shootings of our public officials. I told Tom that as of now I have some leads but nothing solid enough that we could use in a story. I looked at my watch and realized it was two thirty and if I didn't get a move on it I would be late for my three o'clock meeting with Streetwise.

Part 2. Five Smooth Stones

"Never allow yourself to believe that another person's

     misery can contribute to your happiness."
IG

The Punishers

As I walked into Barney's my eyes and nostrils filled with smoke as usual and I could hardly breathe. I fought my way to the rear of the Pub because I knew that was where Streetwise would be sitting facing the door. Streetwise eyes lit up when he saw me and said with a smile, my favorite reporter. I responded jokingly, what's up wise guy, I mean Streetwise. I asked him how he was and what information did he have for me, and was it anything worthy of a trip uptown.

Streetwise stated that the word on the street

was that the group has increased from twenty-five to almost fifty and they are recruiting using the internet and Facebook, especially Snapchat because of how unlikely that it would leave a permanent trail. He stated that they are using coded messages to do their internet recruiting and that they also have foot soldiers that do face to face and one on one recruiting. Streetwise went on to say that he also heard that one or more members of the group attended the last community meeting that was sponsored by the faith leaders and he heard through the grapevine that one or more of them will be at the next meeting hoping to recruit new members. I asked Streetwise how did he hear about the monthly meetings that the faith leaders were sponsoring to help deal with the violence in the neighborhoods. Streetwise responded jokingly that he specializes in knowing what's going down in his town. I responded, so it's your town. I said sarcastically, okay mayor Streetwise, give me a call when you have details and specific information about who is committing these crimes. I gave him a hundred dollars and left the pub and headed home for the day.

One of the other perks that come with my position as a journalist is that I can work from just about any location where there is an internet connection, especially the comfort of my home. I have to admit that my investigation in to these assassinations of New York City judges and politicians was starting to weigh on me because I wasn't making the progress I was hoping for.

The next community meeting was going to be held four days from today. In the meantime, it was Friday afternoon so I decided I would start my weekend early so that I could spend tomorrow revisiting all four locations where the shootings took place and on Sunday I would rest and relax and so that I would be mentally and emotionally refreshed for work on Monday.

Even though there are numerous perks that comes with being a journalist there is also a down side. The down side is when you have the opportunity to uncover a front page story but you can't get the details and factual information you need to write the story it can be frustrating.

Saturday morning came and while I was visiting the four locations where the assassinations took place I had this strange feeling as if someone was watching and following me. I took some pictures at the four locations that I would examine closer upon returning home. At home I studied the photos closely using a magnifying glass but there wasn't anything unusual or out of the ordinary that stood out in the photos. I was glad that Sunday finally came because at least for one day I could put work aside and focus my attention on something relaxing rather than continuing to focus on this bizarre and baffling story.

Isaac Gavin

On Monday morning as I rode the train to work I thought about what my coworkers would be sharing about the shootings and also what they would be expecting from me. I wasn't looking forward to sharing with them that my sources have left me high and dry in a stalled position with nothing new about the investigation.

At the morning meeting everyone was given an opportunity to share anything new and important regarding who was behind the assassinations. Fortunately for me I didn't look to bad or felt awkward because no one else had anything new or fresh to bring to the table. Jerry stressed the fact that we need to get motivated and pick up the pace in finding new sources to help us bring to light this story before the competition beat us to it. He gave all of us an increase in our expense accounts so that we could offer our sources more money to motivate them to if necessary take greater risks to help us crack this story. Jerry went on to stress that we need this story on the front page and that won't happen until we know who's behind the shootings. All of us knew how big this story was and how important it was to get it in our newspaper first before the competition or any other major media.

I inform Jerry and my co-workers that tomorrow night was the first Tuesday of the month and that the faith leaders would be having their monthly community meeting and that they were welcome to join me in attending the meeting. None of my coworkers volunteered to attend the meeting with me.

Tuesday came and I was looking forward to the meeting because I was going to ask the faith leaders if I could speak briefly to the audience and also allow me to interview each of them at their church, temple or synagogue, or their home if they were more comfortable there. The meeting start time is seven o'clock but I decided that I would arrive at the meeting thirty minutes early so that I could mingle and get a feel for the residents that was attending the meeting and maybe meet a new contact.

The God I Never Knew

At seven o'clock all the faith leaders were seated on the stage as the crowd of about three hundred settled in to their seats. Rabbi Belenky stepped up to the podium and asked the group for their attention and welcomed them and thanked them for coming. He went on to say a prayer in the Hebrew language and then interpreted it to English. "May God Bless You And Keep You, May God Make His Face To Shine On You And Give You His Peace." Then Rabbi Belenky introduce Imam Abdullah who came to the podium and thanked everyone for coming and said a prayer in Arabic and then interpreted it to English, O' Allah, Unite Our Hearts And Set Aright Our Mutual Affairs, Guide Us In The Path Of Peace. Next Imam Abdullah introduced Father Gage, who thanked everyone for coming and prayed, "Immaculate Heart Of Mary, Help Us To Conquer The Menace Of Evil Which So Easily Takes Root In The Hearts Of The People Of Today And Whose Immeasurable Effects Already Weigh Down Upon Our Modern World." Father Gage then introduced, Pastor Hammond who thanked the group for coming and prayed, "You Are Keeper O Lord, The Shade On Our Right Hand. Protect Us From Evil And Keep Our Soul. Guard Our Going Out And Our Coming In From This Time And Forever, In Jesus Name, Amen."

Pastor Hammond went on to say that we as faith leaders know that the reason you took the time to come out to the meeting is because of your concern for the violence in our communities and our neighborhoods. He stated that for this reason we as faith leaders have put our difference aside and have invited some specials guests who work for you and share our and your concern for safe communities. The first guest we would like to introduce and bring to the podium is Councilman James Winn.

Councilman Winn introduced himself and told the group that as a public servant he is committed to ensuring that our neighborhoods and schools will be safe and that he would be pushing to get increase police presence on the streets. Rabbi Belenky returned to the podium and said that he would like to introduce their second guess who works tirelessly to keep our streets safe.

When Police Captain William Henson approached the podium half of the audiences began booing him. Captain Henson asked the crowd to please give him a chance to speak and share with them what he hope to do in the near future. The audience finally quieted and he went on to say that his plan is to push for body cameras for all officers and to petition for more accountability from all officers under his command.

Earlier before the meeting started I had an opportunity to get permission from the leaders to say a few words. Imam Abdullah introduced me and told the group that I was a reporter from the Manhattan Times. I approached the podium and thanked the leaders for allowing me to speak. I inform the audience that I was specifically working on a story related the latest shootings of four of New York city public officials and if anyone had information about who was behind these incidents I would find a way to make it worth their while and they would be helping to make the city safer. Someone yelled from the audience, "I don't trust newspapers or the news, they always twist the truth." I told the crowd thank you for letting me speak and that I would be near the front entrance if anyone wanted to speak to me or had questions.

Each of the faith leaders shared a brief encouraging message with the group and each leader invited the audience to attend worship services at their church, synagogue or temple on Sunday. Rabbi Belenky thanked everyone for coming and told them that it was important that they keep coming and to invite their neighbors. As everyone was leaving a young woman approximately twenty-five years old approached me and discreetly slip a piece of paper in my hands and whispered, I have information that could be helpful, and walked away quickly. I decided not to look at the piece of paper yet because I don't think anyone noticed her slipping me the paper and I didn't want anyone to know that she had done so. It was obvious by her body language that she didn't want anyone seeing her communicating with me.

When I got home about nine that night I looked at the piece of paper and on it was the name Dee with a phone number. I was tempted to dial the number but I decided to wait until the next day. The following day around three in the afternoon I decided to call Dee hoping she in fact had some helpful information for me. The phone ranged about seven times and as I was about to hang up a voice came on the line and said hello. I said hello is this Dee from the faith leaders meeting last night? She responded, yes, this is she, who's this? Terry Carter, the journalist from the meeting last night.

The Anointed Assassin

I understand that you have some information about who has been assassinating public officials over the past couple of months. She stated that she knew some people who know some people involved but she was not comfortable talking about it over the phone. I asked Dee if she was familiar with Barney's Pub on Eighth Avenue and Fifty Ninth? She chuckled and said yes, all the so call informants, or should I say information sources hang out there. I asked her if she would be willing to meet me there tomorrow at 3pm. She responded that she would be there and asked did I mean what I said about making it worth her while for information. I chuckled and said, I'm a journalist and I work for a newspaper, we never lie. She responded, well okay then, I will see you tomorrow at three and she hung up the phone.

The next day while at work I thought about the statement Dee made about knowing some people that know some people that could be involved and exactly what did she mean by that statement. As of now all my sources had given me general information but nothing solid with specifics and details. My hope was that with Dee things would be different. The question came to my mind whether any or all of my sources knew each other and if this had become for them just a hustle and a way to make a quick buck or were they supplying legitimate information.

Wade In The Water

The next morning during our 10am morning meeting I could tell by the look on Jerry's face that he was not in a good mood. As we all took our seats around the conference table Susan jokingly stated, if looks could kill one of us if not all of would be dead. Looking in Jerry direction, she asked, did everyone have their morning cup of joe. Jerry gave her a hard stare without responding to her comment. With frustration in his voice, he asked, I need someone at this table to tell me what I want to hear and what I need to hear.

All of us at the table knew exactly what he was referring to. There was dead silence in the room for about thirty seconds before I cleared my throat and shared that I attended the faith leaders meeting on Tuesday night and that there were a few interesting guest speakers in attendance. After sharing the list of speakers that was there I went on to tell them that the faith leaders gave me an opportunity to speak to the group and do some source recruiting. I went on to tell them that I was able to make contact with a young woman who I would be meeting this afternoon. I shared that this contact stated that she knows some people that know some people that are responsible for the crimes against the city's public officials. Jerry responded with the question, does this lead look promising or are you going to be chasing your tail?

I answered, you know this business better than I do, only time will tell. In an angry tone while slamming his fist on the desk, Jerry raised his voice, almost yelling, okay who else has what? Silenced went over the room again.

In a threatening tone, Jerry asked who at this table like their jobs and got up and walked out of the room. Everyone in the room was speechless and we stared at each other for a moment before getting up and exiting the conference room. I went back to my office thinking about Jerry's statement about who likes their job. I started thinking, would he go as far as firing one of us or all of us for not getting enough information about the shootings.

It was now 11am and after an unproductive office meeting I decided I would call my mom and dad and my sister. It's been a week since I've spoken with them and I know my mom would be happy to hear from me. After spending an hour on the phone with family I decided to walk to the deli around the corner and take a lunch break.

While seated in the deli I could hear the sirens blasting and then one after another police, fire trucks, and ambulances came flying by the deli. In all total it must of been twenty or more police cars and emergency vehicles that went pass the deli. I thought to myself, what on God's green earth is going on now. My intentions were to get out of my office and relax in the deli and enjoy my lunch break. Because of all the commotion it was obvious something newsworthy had just happened. I asked for my order to go and rushed back to the office.

As soon as I got off the elevator on the third floor I could see Tom, the assistant manager, waving his hands and summoning me to the conference room. There were police scanners located throughout the building so that we would be aware of all the police and emergency communications. As I walked in the conference room I could tell by the look on everyone's face that whatever just happened wasn't good. Jerry choking on his words stated that congressman Steve Willis was shot once in the back of the head and is being rushed to Manhattan General. He went on to say that it happened around noon time in broad day light while he was using the bathroom at a local restaurant. Unfortunately, there was a back door to the restaurant and as of now there is no identity or description of the assailant.

Jerry stated that the location of the shooting is at Madison Avenue and 42nd Street and that he needed me and Tom to go to the location ASAP to see what we can find out. I reminded Jerry that it was now one thirty and that earlier in the meeting I informed him that I had a meeting with a source at 3pm which is in the opposite direction. Jerry responded, okay, you go meet your source and Susan you accompany Tom to the location where the shooting occurred. I could tell by the look on Susan's face she was not pleased with that arrangement because it was rumored that the two of them vehemently disliked each other.

Lisa got up from the table and went over to the television and turned it on to the news. Across the screen was the words, "Breaking News". The newscaster went on to report that Congressman Willis had been shot once and that he died in the ambulance on the way to the hospital. I immediately thought about the two plastic coins that I found and the unidentified object the police found at the scenes of the shootings. A part of me wanted to go with Tom but I knew it would be better to wait until the following day when the crime scene investigators would not be present. Even though it would still be considered a crime scene tomorrow, I would probably be able to get close enough or even be able to enter the bathroom to search and see if a similar coin or object was left at the scene.

The news reporter went on to say that Congressman Willis was forty-eight years old and leaves behind to mourn his death his wife Laura of twenty-four years and their three children, son Stephen Junior, twenty-four, daughter Cindy, twenty-one, and son Phillip, eighteen. Jerry asked Lisa to turn the television off for a minute because there was something he needed to say. Jerry stated that first we need to keep Congressman Willis's family in our prayers and secondly we need to find out who the hell is behind these shootings, and we need to find out now, not next week. The meeting ended so I went to my office to make a few last minute calls before heading out to meet my latest source, Dee.

Light Inside The Darkness

During the taxi ride to Barney's Pub to meet Dee I speculated about what kind of information she may have and what amount of compensation would she be expecting. As my taxi pulled up to the pub I could see Dee standing near the side door smoking a cigarette. As I exited the taxi in front of the pub I called her named and I could tell she was startled and I got the impression she wanted to run away. Immediately I reminded her who I was and she responded, oh Terry, the newspaper guy from the meeting. I answered yep, chuckling, because when you write the news, you must always tell the truth. I reached out and shook her hands and invited her inside.

As we walked inside I decided to allow Dee to take the lead because I was curious to see if she would take a seat in the back facing the door. And just like Streetwise and Cosmos she took a seat in the back facing the door. I asked her if she wanted me to order her something to drink or did she

The Anointed Assassin

wanted to dive right into the reason for our meeting. She responded that she was okay and wanted to know what questions did I have for her.

I asked her was she aware of what happened downtown just a few hours ago. She responded, no I'm not aware of anything unusual that happen today. She asked, was it something bad, was it another shooting? I responded, unfortunately yes. I informed Dee that around noon today in a restaurant bathroom in the downtown area Congressman Willis was shot once in the head and died in the ambulance on the way to the hospital. Dee gasped and put her hand over her mouth and said, no they didn't. I respond, no who didn't? Dee answered that the people I know that know some of the individuals that are involved in a group that call themselves, "Enough Is Enough".

Dee asked me, how many of the faith leaders meetings have I attended in the past? I responded that I had only attend two, why? She declared that from what she has been told that one or more of the perpetrators committing these crimes attend the meetings every week. I asked her how many of the faith leaders meeting has she attend and who at the meeting did she know personally or have a personal relationship with. She responded that a couple of her neighbors attend the meetings and one coworker that live near her.

I told Dee that I needed her to look me in the eye and answer a question. Who did she think was targeting New York city politicians and judges and why? I told Dee that I needed her to be specific and name names if she knew them. Dee responded, Terry, do you know what you are asking me. If these people are willing to assassinate five New York city judges and politicians, and some in broad daylight, what do you think they would do to me if word got back to them that I spoke with a reporter. Dee went on to say that the best that she could do is point me in the right direction. She stated that if I keep attending the Faith Leaders meeting and watch and listen there would be clues to reveal who is a member of the group Enough Is Enough by the way they dress.

Dee asked, is it true that journalist have a moral, ethical, and legal duty to protect their sources. I answered yes, your name will not be shared, not even with my coworkers. I asked Dee was their anything else she could tell me or anyone else that she could point me to. Dee stated that depending on how she was compensated for the current information she already provided she may have the names of the leaders at our next meeting. For some reason, and I'm not sure why, her information sounded credible. Something in my gut was telling me she was on to something. I gave her two hundred dollars, a hundred more than what I gave Streetwise or Cosmos because I believed her when she told me that some of the answers were at the Faith Leaders meetings. I thanked Dee for the

The Anointed Assassin

information and we exited the Pub together and went in separate directions.

It was almost the end of the of the work day so I hop in a cab and headed home. As of now I have heard three different versions of who is behind the shootings. Of the three versions given by Cosmos, Streetwise and Dee, I found Dee's story to be more compelling. That night while lying in bed I kept wondering about the possibility of a coin being left at the scene of Congressman Willis shooting similar to the one left at the other shootings. I decided that since the location where the shooting took place may still be an active crime scene I would wait and go there early tomorrow morning to search to see if a coin was left at the scene.

There was also one additional contact, Styx, that I hadn't reached out to in quite some time. Maybe he could shed light on some information that would line up with and hopefully confirm one of the other sources information. After a restless night I got up at 5am, got dressed and headed to the scene where Congressman Willis was shot. When I arrived at the restaurant, which was in a hotel lobby, there was still police tape covering the bathroom. Luckily for me the clerk at the front desk could not see around the corner to the entrance of the bathroom from her position. While the hotel clerk was helping a guess I snuck around the corner and ducked under the police tape and went into the bathroom. Because this was a large hotel and a large bathroom there were several sinks, urinals, and stalls for me to look under, around, and search behind. After about five minutes of searching and close to giving up a thought came to my mind to move the trash can.

Bingo, there it was. A coin just like the previous two I had already found with the dove on one side and two capital A's on the opposite side. I picked up the coin and stared at it for a while before slipping it into my pocket and quietly easing out of the bathroom. I stood at the bathroom entrance and peep around the corner at the front desk to make sure the clerk was engage with someone and not looking in my direction. Fortunately for me the clerk was looking down taking a hotel guest information.

There was one person that did see me come out from the bathroom and lift up the yellow police tape to go under. There was a little boy about five years old staring in my direction while pulling on his mother's jacket trying to get her to look in my direction. I immediately put my finger over my lips giving him the sign to keep quiet and not give me away. The boy with his eyes locked on me slowly dropped his hands to his side while I eased out the front door of the hotel.

I jumped into a taxi that was waiting in front of the hotel and headed in to work.

Dis-Connecting The Dots

After finding three coins at three different crime scenes it was clear that the same person or persons was responsible for these shootings. I wrestled with the thought of whether it was time to share this information about the coins with my coworkers or not. I wanted this story to be credited to me and me alone. After five years of working here I'm starting to get a better understanding how this newspaper and news reporting business works. I've heard stories around the office about coworkers stealing one another's ideas and leads from their coworkers who was naive and shared too much information with someone they thought they could trust.

It was still early when I arrived at work so rather than going upstairs to my office I decided to go across the street to Starbucks and get a coffee and a bagel. While sitting in Starbucks drinking my coffee and staring out the window I thought about whether I was putting myself in any danger by digging into who is behind these assassinations. Unfortunately, every year to many journalists have been killed or seriously injured in their pursuit of getting an exclusive story, especially those journalists who have been captured by terrorist groups and those who were covering military conflicts. It is a well-known fact that over ninety-four journalists were killed last year while attempting to cover stories that were considered controversial.

I finished my coffee and my depressing reflection on the downside of being a journalist and headed across the street to my office to do some research and make a few phone calls. After an unproductive morning of research and phone calls that were answered by machines, I decided to reach out to Styx, one of my first contacts when I first became a journalist. Up until now I have heard three different versions of who is behind these shootings and I'm hoping Styx's information will confirm and match one of them. I picked up the phone and dialed Styx number hoping that his number was still active since it has been almost two years since I've spoken to him. The telephone rung at least ten times before I finally heard a voice on the other end that I honestly didn't recognize, so I asked to speak to Styx. The voice on the other end of the phone responded sharply, who's this? I answered, Terry Carter with the New York Times. Styx slowly and hesitantly said, this is Styx and I'm not sure I want to continue this conversation Terry.

Surprised by Styx's response I asked him why he wasn't sure about speaking to me, was it something I did or didn't do? He responded that it wasn't me as much as it was them. I said them who? Almost in a whisper with fear in his voice, Styx responded, so I guess you haven't heard the news about Cosmos. I ask Styx what happened to Cosmos? Styx stated that Cosmos was found shot to death in front of his apartment building with a note on his body saying, you should of kept your mouth shut and mind your own business.

Initially I couldn't believe what I was hearing, so I asked Styx, was he sure that it was Cosmos? Styx responded, you are the newspaper man you should know how to verify information. I told Styx that he was right and that I would google it after we hung up. I asked Styx did he know what Cosmos real name is? He answered yes, that its Ronald Wiggins. Before I could ask him what did he know about the assassinations of the politicians Styx quickly said, Terry I hate to disappoint you but all of a sudden I have developed a severe case of amnesia and I would appreciate it if you don't call me for another two years. Styx stated that I will leave you with this thought, from what I have heard, these people are serious and they are dangerous and I want no part of having to deal with them and he hung up the phone without saying goodbye.

Stunned by Styx response and trepidation, I listened to the dial tone for a few seconds before hanging up the phone and reclining in my seat thinking about the news I just heard. I googled the name Ronald Wiggins and his name popped up with information about his death and how he was murdered. I sat at my desk thinking about the fact that some people death is front page news and others don't even make the last page of the paper.

I decided that I would call Cosmos girlfriend to verify that Cosmos and Ronald Wiggins was in fact the same person and if so offer her my condolences. I dialed Cosmos number and his girlfriend answered on the first ring with a soft, sad and sobbing voice. I said hello and told her who I was and before I could tell her I was sorrow to hear about what happen to Cosmos she started screaming on the phone that it was my fault and that she hoped they do the same thing to me and slammed the phone down in my ear. I thought to myself, two hang ups in two minutes, maybe it was time to share the information with my coworkers about the coins.

With the body count piling up I started having second thoughts about whether I should pursue this story any further. All of a sudden I had a thousand thoughts running through my head and most of them filled me with fear and anxiety. One of the thoughts that kept repeating itself in my mind was what Cosmos's girlfriend said about my actions being responsible for Cosmos death. And even more dreadful than the thought of being responsible for Cosmos death was the frightful thought of and the possibility of the same thing happening to me.

It was near the end of the work day so I decided to sleep on the thought of whether it was time to share the information with my coworkers. Unfortunately, I tossed and turned all night because the decision to share this information could possibly put others in the crosshairs of the perpetrators of these violent and brutal assassinations. Yet on the other hand if I didn't share what I knew with someone and something was to happen to me how would they know what direction to look in for answers.

The next morning as I was in my kitchen having coffee and watching the morning news the reporter stated that an attempt was made on Councilman Fred Greene life last night around 8:30pm while he was walking his dog. The news reporter stated that the suspect was interrupted in his attempt by a security person who was watching the Councilman from his car about hundred yards away. The suspect was able to get a shot off that struck the Councilman in the leg before the security person was able to return fire at the perpetrator not knowing whether he hit the suspect or not. The security person said while sitting in his car he noticed someone approaching the Councilman suspiciously and by the time he was able to get to councilman he noticed the suspect reaching into his coat pulling out a weapon and firing once before he was able to return fire.

The security person said he gave chase but the suspect was able to elude him through and alley and jumped into the passenger side of a dark colored SUV that sped off quickly. Councilman Greene was treated at Manhattan General for a flesh wound and was kept overnight for observation. Both the Councilman and the security person said they could not give a clear description of the suspect, except that he was white, about six feet tall, approximately two hundred pounds, and wearing dark glasses. The security person stated that during the chase of the suspect that he noticed that he dropped a small item that later turned out to be a plastic coin which was turned over to the police department.

After hearing the news report about Councilman Greene along with what I found out about Cosmos, and the information I received from Styx, I knew that it was time to share what I had uncovered with my coworkers. One of my concerns at this point was how would they feel towards me because I kept the information to myself for more than a two months.

As soon as I walked in the building I nervously headed toward Jerry's office trying to think of the right words to tell him that I have important information that I think needs to be shared with the team immediately.

As I approached Jerry's door I stopped momentarily frozen in my tracks because I started having second thoughts about what I should do. I said a quick prayer and I felt something in my spirit telling me it was time because I could be in danger and not telling them could put them in the same danger.

No More Secrets

I tapped on Jerry's door lightly and leaned my head in as he was picking up the phone to make a call. I said to Jerry, before you make your call there was something important that I needed to share with him and I believe he would agree that the entire team may need to know as well. Jerry responded that whatever it is I can tell by the look on your face that it's weighing heavy on you. Jerry invited me into his office and told me to closed the door behind me and have a seat.

I started the conversation by stating that at this point I'm not sure whether I handled what I'm about to tell you in the right manner and If I didn't I offer you and the rest of the team my sincerest apology. Jerry anxiously blurted out well what is it, don't keep me in suspense. Jerry asked whether it was a life or death matter or something that was detrimental to the paper or something that could be used in a liability suit against the paper? I answered no nothing like that.

I told Jerry that while investigating the assassinations of the public officials I received some information through my sources that I have not shared, and that I found an object at the scene of the crimes that I'm confident holds a motive for the crimes. Jerry with his eyes glued on me and his mouth wide open instructed me to go on. I stated that I have been collecting information from three sources that vary in details and yet have some similarities.

My first source, Streetwise, informed me that word on the street was that a group of about twenty-five and growing that go by the name, World Changers, were responsible for the assassinations. My second source, Cosmos, who was assassinated two days ago for talking to me, said that the group responsible go by the name, The Sons of Anarchy, and all of them have serve prison time and have ball heads. My third source, Dee, said that one or more of the perpetrators attend the monthly meetings that is sponsored by the faith leaders. She also stated that the group motto and name is, "Enough Is Enough."

And there is one other important factor I would like to add and that is the plastic coins that I have found at three of the murder scenes and the police has found two similar coins at the other crime scenes. Jerry asked did I have the coins with me or in my office. I answered no, the coins were at my apartment hidden in my dresser draw. Jerry asked me to describe the coin for him. I told him that they were hard gold colored plastic coins with two capitals A's on one side and a dove on the opposite side.

The Anointed Assassin

Jerry rubbed his hands together and ask me how long have I been sitting on this information and what were my reasons for not sharing it sooner with him and the rest of the team? I dropped my head and then looked up at Jerry and answered that I was afraid of not getting the proper respect and credit for my work. I went on to say that because I was the least senior member of the Insight Team that I assume that I would have to turn over my leads and sources to a senior reporter who would get praise and respect for the work. I apologize again to Jerry and told him one of my dreams and aspirations is to write a Pulitzer Prize story and I thought this was that opportunity.

Jerry asked, are you certain that your source Cosmos was killed because of sharing information about a group that might be responsible for the assassinations? I answered yes, there was a note left with his body about why he was killed and his girlfriend screamed at me on the phone that he was killed because he talked to me and she hope the same thing would happen to me. I told Jerry that I hope that he was not upset at me for withholding this information and going forward I promised to make sure he and the rest of the team are aware of any pertinent information as soon as I uncover it.

I asked Jerry did he think that we needed to have an office meeting as soon as possible to share what I've uncovered with the team. Jerry responded by asking me, did I think that myself or my other sources, or the Insight Team could be in any danger. Rubbing my sweaty palms and choking on my words, I responded that I didn't know for sure but I have this uncomfortable feeling in my gut that tells me we need to be extra vigilant. In other word Jerry, as the saying goes, it's better to be safe rather than sorry. I told Jerry that I also think that in addition to sharing this with the team, we need to set up a meeting with the police department and share the information with them also.

I told Jerry that I had met a Detective Harrison during the investigation of Judge Barrows shooting because it happened near my apartment building. And that I also went by the fourth precinct and had a conversation with Detective Smith after Councilman Ford was killed because I heard they found a coin similar to the one I found. In addition to that, Captain William Henson spoke at the last Faith Leaders meeting about ways to keep the streets and the neighborhoods safe.

Jerry agreed that the first thing that needed to be done is to have an emergency meeting with the team this morning and bring them up to speed on the latest developments.

Jerry slid his chair up to his computer and began to type an email to the other members of the team informing them that we would be having a meeting in the conference room in thirty minutes. I informed Jerry that I needed to go by my office to make a phone call and grab some of my notes and that I would meet them in the conference room at 9am.

I sat down at desk and put my hands over my face and leaned back in my chair wondering how will this whole thing play out with my coworkers and the police. A thousand thoughts were racing through my head. Am I in danger, were any of my coworkers in danger, was my family in danger, or were any of my other sources in danger. I decided that I would call Dee and Streetwise to informed them about what happen to Cosmos and remind them to be careful and watch their backs.

I dialed Dee's number but the call went straight to voice mail. I left a message on her voice mail for her to call me as soon as possible and that it was urgent and important. Next I dialed Streetwise number and he answered hello on the first ring. I proceeded to tell him who I was but he interrupted me and stated I know who this is and shouted, what's up newspaper man. I asked him how he was and stated that there were some important developments that has transpired since we last talk and I asked him did he hear anything new on the streets about the assassinations and about what happened to Cosmos? With some hesitancy in his voice and in a whisper Streetwise asked, what happened to Cosmos?

I told Streetwise I didn't want him to panic and I asked him not to hang up the phone after I tell him what I'm about to share with him. Streetwise answered with a long okay. I told him that it seems from early reports that Cosmos was assassinated for sharing information with me about the activities of a group he thought was involved in what happened to the public officials. Streetwise asked, how do you know he was killed for that reason. I answered that a note was left with his body telling the reason for what was done to him. Streetwise responded oh, and went silent. I spoke into the phone, are you still there? Streetwise answered, yes I'm still here but I can't say for how long hearing what I just heard.

    I asked Streetwise did he know Cosmos personally? He answered that they were not close friends but that the two of them had cross each other's path once or twice. He went on to say that most of the people that do what they do know of each other because they travel in the same circles seeking the same information which most of us accept can be dangerous at times. I asked Streetwise, in addition to knowing Cosmos, did he know Styx and a young lady by the name of Dee? He responded that he was familiar with Styx and had met him once at Wally's Pub but that he didn't know who Dee was. I told Streetwise that I spoke to Styx recently and he was aware of what happened to Cosmos and told me never to contact him again. So my question to you Streetwise is, do you intend to go off the radar or will it continue to be business as usual between us? Streetwise

The Anointed Assassin

chuckled and said, for me, it's always business as usual, indicating that he could not afford to go off the radar because this was who he was come what may.

I thanked Streetwise for all the help he had given me over the years and reminded him to be careful and that I would be in touch with him soon and that I would be extra generous the next time we meet.

Just as I hung up the phone my coworker Lisa leaned her head in my office and stated that Jerry and the rest of the team were waiting in the conference room for me to join them. I looked at my watch and realized that forty minutes had past so I was ten minutes late for our office meeting. I gathered up my notes and followed Lisa down to the conference room. As I walked in the conference room I could see the anticipation on everyone face because Jerry announced that it was mandatory that everyone attend. I said good morning to everyone and apologized for being late and sat down in the seat next to Jerry.

Jerry opened the meeting by apologizing for calling a mandatory meeting with such a short notice but because of what was at stake it was necessary to do so. He went on to say that both himself and I had critical information to share related to the assassinations of the public officials. Jerry asked me to share the information with the team that I shared with him earlier and after I was finished he would give instruction as to how we should proceed going forward. I repeated to the team everything that I had shared with Jerry earlier and as I was doing so I could feel the eyes in the room locked on me like lasers that were penetrating my entire being. After I was finished a deafening silence fell over the room for about sixty seconds that felt like an eternity.

Finally, with a bit of sarcasm in his voice, Tom asked, so what made you decide to come forward now rather than earlier when you first uncovered the information. Stan put his hand over his mouth and cough, and softly stated, sound like someone's is scared to me. Jerry looked over at Stan with a glare in his eyes and said, I think you need to apologize to Terry. I quickly told Jerry and Stan that it wasn't a problem, that no apology was necessary, and yes, I was scared.

Susan asked, do you think that the people who killed Cosmos know where you work? I responded that I wasn't sure but that his girlfriend said he was killed because he shared information about those responsible for the assassinations. I added that I don't know how far a reach these people have and since they are bold enough to kill politicians in broad day light they could hurt one of us as well. Everyone in the room except Jerry shouted, one of us at the same time.

Jerry raised his hands and told everyone to calm down and let's not get carried away. Stan, in

The Anointed Assassin

his squeaky and gay voice, answered, what do you mean calm down. He reminded Jerry that four politicians were dead and one of Terry's source so our response was only a natural reaction. Jerry stated that he understood everyone's fears and concerns and that he would do everything in his power to insure that we were safe and protected. He went on to say that he would schedule another meeting soon and would arrange to have one or more police officers sit in and also have them assign a detail to keep an eye on our location. Jerry ended the meeting by telling everyone to be careful and to keep their eyes and ears open, and if we saw or hear anything suspicious to report it to him or security immediately.

As we were leaving the conference room Jerry tap me on my shoulder and whispered in my ear that he wanted me to stay so he could have a word alone with me.

After everyone had left the room Jerry stated that he was both somewhat disappointed in me for holding back the information but at the same time proud of the work I had done to get the information.

Jerry put his hand on my shoulder and looked me in the eyes and stated that it was imperative that going forward every piece of information I uncover that is related to these assassinations is to be shared speedily and that I should bring the coins to his office tomorrow. I assured Jerry that I would do just that and I would prefer bringing one of the coins and leaving the other at home. Jerry nodded that that was acceptable.

Part 3. At The Red Sea

"Whenever you feel the need to prove yourself to

someone you are in some form of bondage"...IG

Saved By The Bell

I returned to my office and sat at my desk thinking I had just dodge a bullet because I did think Jerry and the team would be upset to the point where I could of lost my job.

I picked up my office phone to check my messages and the first message made me slam the phone down. I didn't want to believe what I just heard. I sat frozen for a moment with my heart pounding against my chest trying to convince myself that I made a mistake about the message I just heard. I worked up the courage to pick up the phone and listen to the message a second time. I was not imagining things. The growling voice on the other end of the phone stated that if I wanted to live to see twenty-eight I would be wise to end my investigation into the assassinations. I hung up the phone and thought to myself how did this person know who I was, where I worked, and most disturbing, that I would be twenty-eight my next birthday.

All of a sudden I felt like I had been caught in a category five hurricane. I had just promised Jerry that I would be forthcoming and transparent about everything going forward but how do you tell your boss someone just threatened your life.

I prayed about it for a moment and something inside of me said that I should inform Jerry about the call. I realized that the decisions I was making to continue investigating this story was moving me in to uncharted waters and eventually I could cross over into the twilight zone. I was determined to uncover who was responsible for these murders even if it cost me my job but hopefully not my life.

I immediately got up from my desk and headed towards Jerry's office thinking to myself what can of worms have I just opened. I walked into Jerry's office without knocking, closed the door and sat down. With his eyes locked on me Jerry stated that I was white as a sheet as if I had just seen a ghost.

Fighting to get the words out, I responded that what I just heard on my voice mail is a lot scarier than a ghost. Jerry asked, what was the message that I heard on my voice mail. I answered that a male voice informing me that if I wanted to see my next birthday that I'd better stop investigating the assassinations. Jerry stood up from his chair and ask me how many messages like that one did I receive. I answered that after hearing the first message I hung up the phone and that I wasn't sure if there are others. Jerry told me to make sure I don't erase the message and that we needed to file a police report and arrange a prompt meeting with law enforcement on both the state and federal level.

I reminded Jerry about my previous conversations with both a Detective Harrison and Detective Smith and that I had their business cards and contact information. Jerry suggested that I call both of them from his office now and arrange to meet with them tomorrow morning around 10am at our location.

Luckily, I was able to reach both detectives and they both agreed to meet with our team the following morning.

After I hung up the phone Jerry suggested that I bring both coins tomorrow and turn them over to the detectives. I reluctantly agreed to do so because I was hoping to keep one as a souvenir.

The following morning our entire team met with Detective Harrison and Detective Smith and I explained what information I uncovered from

The Anointed Assassin

my sources, explained why Cosmos was killed, showed them the coins, and let them listen to the threatening message on my voice mail. Both detectives reprimanded me for not contacting law enforcement sooner concerning what I uncovered and the coins I found. I apologized to both of them for my actions and promised nothing like this would ever happen again. They reminded me of the number of public officials that had already been killed by this vigilante group including one of my contacts and that we shouldn't take any unnecessary chances. Before leaving both detectives gave each of us their business cards and told us that they would have a squad car keep an eye on our location, and before leaving asked, if we had any questions?

I slowly raised my hand and asked the officers was the item that was found at the scene of Councilman Ford's assassination also a coin like the coins I gave them. Both detectives looked at each other and hesitated for a few seconds before Detective Smith answered that they would prefer not to answer that question at this time, then both officers walked out the conference room. Before leaving the conference room Jerry reminded us that we should be careful, watch our backs, keep our eyes and ears open, and to report anything suspicious immediately.

As I walked back to my office I realized that I was

at a crossroad and had to decide whether I wanted to continue with the investigation or cower back with fear and walk away. I thought about contacting my parents and getting their opinion about whether I should or shouldn't continue the investigation.

I sat at my desk and worked up the courage to listen to the remaining messages on my voicemail. Thankfully the one message I heard earlier was the only threatening message that was left on my voicemail. It was Friday afternoon and because of all the stress and strain of everything that transpired over the past few says I decided to leave work early. I needed to find something or someone to help me relax and take the edge off. I decided to stop by Wally's Pub and have a beer or maybe something stronger and hopefully I would run in to Streetwise or Dee.

The next Faith Leaders meeting was coming up on Tuesday and I thought about asking Stan to attend the meeting with me.

Even though my parents were regular church goers and made me and my siblings say grace over our meals I wasn't one who was big on faith. Because I was feeling a knot in my stomach and my palms were sweaty from the fear that now had become a reality in my life, I was willing to try anything, even praying to try to calm my nerves.

After having a couple of beers I decide to head

home thinking about what my next move would be to unravel this mystery.

It has been almost a year since I had seen my parents so maybe visiting them could be just the thing I need to get my thoughts back on track.

I was able to book a late flight Friday night and a return flight Sunday night to visit my parents.

It was refreshing to see them and I received and extra blessing because both my brother and sister was also visiting them.

It was now Sunday evening and time to return to the big apple so my family reminded me that Carter's never quit because of fear so I needed to get back to the drawing board and finish investigating these assassinations.

The first thing I needed to take care that Monday morning when I returned to New York was to try convincing Stan to come with me to the Faith Leaders meeting tomorrow night.

As I approach Stan's office I noticed the door was closed an upon knocking received no answer. It was early Monday morning and Stan has made it a habit of coming in late on Monday and Friday mornings. As I turn to walk away Tom shouted down the hall that Stan informed him that he would be coming into work around 11am.

Coming In From The Rain

I went back to my office to make some phone calls but first I wanted to check my voicemail to see if there were any other threatening messages like the one that was left a few days earlier.

The first message was from my parents thanking me for the visit and suggesting that I don't let the next visit take a year. The second message was from Dee reminding me about the meeting tomorrow night saying she was looking forward to seeing me there. The third message was a male voice stating that he had firsthand knowledge about the assassinations and wanted to meet privately and discreetly with me alone and no one else.

I sat dumfounded because I didn't know if this was a hoax or the real thing. The message went on to say that if I involved the police or anyone else that he would call it off and I would never hear from him again. The last thing the message said that if I agreed to his terms that he would get a message to me when and where to meet. I hung up the phone without erasing the message.

I immediately thought about the conversations I had both with Stan and the Detectives about being open, honest, and transparent about any future information that I would uncover. I decided that if I was going to make headway in getting to the bottom of who was committing

The Anointed Assassin

these atrocities I would have to risk everything and keep this information from my coworkers and the police and postpone the idea of inviting Stan along to the meeting tomorrow night.

Just as I picked up the phone to call Streetwise Stan stuck his head in my office and ask was I looking for him. I nervously hung up the phone and cleared my throat and answered that it wasn't important and that I just wanted to say good morning. Stan asked, how was your weekend and did I receive any more threatening calls. I hesitated and without looking Stan in the eyes I answered that the only message I received was from my parents thanking me for visiting them. As he was walking away he replied that if I received any more threatening calls or get any messages that was out of the ordinary that I needed to find him immediately. I answered that I would definitely do so.

I picked up the phone and dialed Streetwise number but got his voice mail and left him a message to call me if he had any new information that would be helpful.

The following evening as I walked into the Faith leaders meeting I noticed that the group had grown to twice the number that attended the previous month. To my surprise when I looked across the room there was Dee and Streetwise having a cozy and chummy conversations like they were old friends.

As I approached the two they both gave me the impression that they were glad to see me. After some small talk I asked both of them if they had come across any additional information that could help me unravel the mystery behind who is responsible for the assassinations. Streetwise nodded a sigh indicating no but Dee pointed at her nose indicating that there was something right in front of me that I was missing.

Suddenly there was a voice asking for everyone's attention indicating that the meeting was about to begin. Imam Amir Abdullah thanked everyone for coming and stated that after each Faith Leader had shared there would be an opportunity for the audience to ask questions.

While the Imam was sharing I wasn't sure if it was my imagination but I felt like he was intentionally staring in our direction.

Father Nicolas Cage was the last of the leaders to come to the podium to speak. I wanted to wait until he had finished speaking before going to the restroom but I just could not wait any longer. As I was leaving the bathroom Imam Amir was coming through the door and seem to intentionally bump into me saying excuse me without making eye contact.

Father Gage finished sharing with the group and then informed them that the four leaders would now take questions.

Across the room there was a group of five men who were dressed in black and wearing red, white, and blue bandanas that stood in an area away from everyone else. One of the men raised his hand and said that his question was for all four of the Faith Leaders. He asked that as men of faith do you all think that the recent tragedy that happen to the politicians was justice being served.

Rabbi Belenky stood up and answered that as men of faith we believe in the sanctity of life and only God has the authority to say when someone life should end. One of the other men from the group replied, what about David and Goliath? Pastor Hammond stood up and answered that as the Rabbi has indicated, only God has the authority, and in that particular case He gave David permission, or as some would say, the anointing to do so.

To my surprise Dee raised her hand and asked Father Gage if someone came to him and confessed to being involved in the assassinations of the judges and politicians how would he handle it? He responded that as a Catholic Priest he is obligated to keep a person's confession confidential, nevertheless because of the grievous nature of these crimes he would have to pray and ask for direction.

There were a few more questions from the audience that were irrelevant to why we were there so the leaders thanked everyone for coming and ended the meeting.

The following morning when I arrived at work the first thing I decided to do was check my voice mail for messages. I had one message and it was from the same person who left the previous one indicating he had firsthand information about the assassinations. The message indicated that the number that he was calling from was untraceable and that he would contact me from time to time and provide details once I demonstrate that I can be trusted.

The caller went on to say that the reason he decided to contact me was because his conscious was bothering him because of an experience he had a week ago. The last thing the message said was that he would be in touch with me soon and he hoped that I could be trusted otherwise I might not like what could come next.

I hung up the phone and sat at my desk in a daze wondering what my next move should be. I said a quick prayer and decided that I would continue to keep this information to myself with the hopes of truly writing the Pulitzer Prize story I've always dreamed of doing. There was one of three consequences that could come from this decision, either I would write a great front page story, or lose my job, or even worst, lose my life.

Even though I had caller ID it was impossible for me to get the number that the call came from so I would have to be patient and wait for the next call. In the mean time I wanted to setup a meeting with both Dee and Streetwise together to see what they knew about the five men who was dressed in all black who were at the meeting.

For the next two days I made sure that I didn't make any commitments that would take me away from my desk just in case a call came in from the caller. For two days every time the phone rang I answered it on the first ring hoping to hear the voice of the person who left the message about having firsthand knowledge about the assassinations.

Anonymous

It was Friday three O'clock in the afternoon and I had given up hope of hearing from the caller today and just as I was about to leave the office for the weekend the phone rang. Somehow before I picked up the phone something in my soul told me this was the call I was waiting for. I picked up the phone and put it to my ear and hesitated before nervously saying, hello. The voice on the other end of the phone said, hello Mr. Carter, can I trust you? I answered yes, you can trust me. The caller went on to say that he would like to call me on my private cell number to explain to me why the politicians were eliminated and why he didn't want to be a part of any future assassinations that are being planned.

I said to the caller, so your saying that there are plans in the works to commit more assassinations? He answered yes, and that he didn't want to be a part of it because of a dream and a vision that he recently experienced. The caller went on to say that if the other members of the group find out he was talking to me both of our lives could be in danger. The caller stated that what he wanted to do was to call me when I was at home to ensure that there are no mistakes made by either of us. I responded that it was fine by me and gave him my cell phone number and asked him when was he planning to call. He answered maybe tonight maybe not and the next thing I heard was a dial tone.

Before leaving the office for the weekend I made calls to Dee and Streetwise and arranged for them to meet me at Barney's Pub at 5pm. As I approached the elevator Stan was waiting to get on also. As we rode the elevator down Stan asked was there anything new going on and did I have any special plans for the weekend. I answered, no, nothing new going on and that I was going to relax this weekend and maybe take in a movie with a friend.

As we walked out of the front door of our office building together Stan ask would I like a ride home. Normally I would say yes, but because I was meeting Dee and Streetwise and didn't want him to know about it, I answered no, I was okay.

Stan asked me was I sure because he was visiting a friend in my neighborhood and it wouldn't be out of his way. I answered thank you for the offer but told him I would be making a few stops before going home. He answered okay, then told me to be safe and have a great weekend and that he would see me Monday and turned and went into the parking garage.

Because it was Friday afternoon the traffic in Manhattan was insane so it took a while for my taxi to reached Barney's Pub. When I walked inside the pub it was pack because happy hour on Fridays was from 4pm-7pm. I finally was able work my way through the crowd and reached the back where Dee and Streetwise were both sitting facing the door. I sat down and greeted them both and thanked them for coming.

I asked both Streetwise and Dee what did they know about the five men who were at the faith leaders meeting who were dressed in black and wearing the red, white and blue bandanas? Dee ask me did I think that those men were the ones responsible for the assassinations, then she laughed? I asked her what was funny, and did she think I was way off base? Streetwise chimed in and said that he had seen those guys around and that they were part of a motorcycle club called the Sons Of Anarchy that consisted of about twenty five members. Dee added that she had seen them around and if she was a betting person she would bet against them being the group responsible. I asked Streetwise if he was a betting person how would he bet? He responded that he was a betting person and he could see them being involved because he had seen them in action when they had a conflict with another bike club.

I asked both Dee and Streetwise was there any hard evidence that either of them could share with me to prove their involvement? Both of them answered no. I gave both of them a hundred dollars each and told them that I would give five hundred dollars to the first person who bought information that definitively proves who is behind these assassinations. Streetwise laughed and said, five hundred dead presidents for possibly putting my life on the line. Dee asked, how much money does a newspaper make when it carries a front page story that sells a million copies? I answered that I get where both of them were coming from but unfortunately that is the best offer that I can make.

The three of us got up from the table and walked out the Pub and said our goodbyes and went our separate ways.

On my way home I thought about the statement the caller made about trust. I hoped that by me meeting and talking to Dee and Streetwise that I was not putting myself or them in danger. I didn't know if I or them was being watched or followed.

The Anointed Assassin

Even though I'm comfortable taking New York Public Transit to some destinations, it was Friday evening in New York and after this week events I decided I would be more comfortable taking New York Finest, a yellow cab home.

By the time I arrived at my apartment building it was after dark so I gave the cab driver a large tip and asked him to wait until I was inside the lobby of my building before driving away.

I flopped down on my sofa, turned the television on to the news and thought about the week that had just gone by, especially the strange phone calls. I dozed off and when I woke I realized that I had been sleeping for almost two hours.

I got up from my sofa and went to the kitchen and was about to try to find something for dinner when my cell phone rang. For a minute I froze, then I look at the screen that said caller unknown. I answered, hello. The voice on the other end of the phone said, hello Mr. Carter, are you ready to help me find my way back to the light. I answered, back to the light? He responded, yes, back to the light because over the past three months I have participated in events that come from the darkest evil known to the human soul. I answered, are you referring to the assassinations of the pubic officials? The caller answered yes, them and unfortunately some innocent individuals that my associates thought were detrimental to our goals.

So Mr. Carter that is what brings me to you. The caller stated that he was okay with eliminating the dirty thieving no good self-serving politicians. But when they consented to killing innocent people that was where he drew the line and decided he needed to do something to end this. So Mr. Carter the first call we made to you was to scare you and to get you to back off the investigation. My associates were present so I had to make the threat seem real and convincing. When I made the second call I was alone and that was when I stated that I wanted to meet. But I've decided for the time being that all our communications be done over the phone.

Also, once I started thinking differently I had this dream and a vision that I'm still trying to process and understand.

I Have A Dream

I asked the caller would he be comfortable sharing the dream and the vision with me? The caller answered that he didn't mind sharing the dream. The caller stated that in the dream he was fishing at this lake and suddenly two men dressed in all white came up behind him and grabbed him and pulled him in the water and held him under. I struggled to come up but they held me under so long that I began to lose consciousness. I finally stop struggling and surrendered and they let me go and then all of a sudden they disappeared and I came up out of the water.

As I walked toward the shore I felt this sensation in my heart and soul like I had never felt in my life. I felt like a new person. I felt light, and free, and whole, like I was born anew.

And in the vision I had just gone to bed and I was about to fall asleep when a blood stained cross came down out of the ceiling and disappeared. So Mr. Carter, I'm not sure exactly what it means but I do have some ideas about what message I'm supposed to get from the dream and the vision. Well Mr. Carter, what do you think, do you think I might be losing my mind and need to seek professional help? I told the caller that only he could decide if what he experienced had any real significance or not.

I asked the caller if there was a name, a code, or a handle that I could use when I refer to him. He responded that I should just refer to him as the caller for now. I asked him was he willing to talk about his associates in detail and share some specifics about the group and their activities? He answered that in time he would share more specific details but this call was just make an introduction. He stated that as long as he believes that he could continue to trust me that he would over time share whatever information was needed to stop the assassinations.

The Caller stated that in the beginning he was the one who approached the others with the idea of doing something about the corrupt judges and politicians.

I asked the caller if he has had a change of heart and wanted to expose them and himself, was I correct in assuming that? The caller answered yes, that it was his idea that got all of this started and he feels it was his responsibility to do what is necessary to bring it to an end. He added, I know you may find this hard to believe Mr. Carter, but I am willing to accept whatever punishment that is exacted upon me. I would like to say Mr. Carter that for some reason unbeknownst to me I am not afraid, and something inside of me is telling me not to worry, I will see you through this.

I responded, wow, that is an interesting perspective for someone who if caught could spend the rest of their life in prison, or possibly face the death penalty. The caller chuckled and answered, we all die Mr. Carter and being afraid doesn't change anything.

Caller, I have a question for you, is your associates planning another assassination in the near future and if so how do you plan to stop it? That is where you come in Mr. Carter, I'm hoping together the two of us can come up with a plan to stop them without them finding out that we did so. What I was thinking Mr. Carter, that once they choose the next target I can let you know and you can inform

The Anointed Assassin

the target and/or the authorities. What do you think Mr. Carter, I am open for other ideas? I was speechless for a moment and then said to Caller, I have to give it some thought.

I informed Caller that I needed him to clarify a statement that he made about involving others. I asked Caller did he still insisted that I don't seek advice or counsel from other sources? The caller answered, that is correct Mr. Carter, for now I would prefer that no one else has any information related to our communications. He stated that the reason for him taking this position is that the less people who is privy to this information the less people he has put in potential danger.

The caller went on to say that once we get this resolved and my associates are no longer a threat that he would give me information and details that would become one of the biggest stories in the twenty first century. Caller, can I ask you a another question, since you approach the others with the idea of eliminating crooked and dirty judges and politicians, then why don't you approach them with the idea of ending it? The caller answered, believe it or not Mr. Carter I did do just that and they strongly rejected the idea of ending it.

As a matter of fact, Mr. Carter, one of the other members approach me privately telling me that the other members were concerned about my commitment to the goals of the group. If my associates come to believe that I am not a hundred percent with them then I could be eliminated. And if they caught wind that I am talking to you Mr. Carter then you could also be eliminated. So Mr. Carter I have to do an academy award winning job of acting to keep convincing them that I'm fully committed until this whole thing is behind us.

So Mr. Carter, before I say goodnight I need to ask you a question, after hearing an extract of what my life has become do you think that you would be comfortable working with me until this nightmare is over. I answered that I had to admit that this is a lot to digest and process, nevertheless, I'm a journalist and in order to get to the truth or expose corruption one has to be willing to step out of his or her comfort zone. So my answer to your question Caller is yes, I'm committed to bringing the truth to light and to helping end these senseless murders.

Caller, I have a question for you before you hang up, would you explain the significance of the plastic coins with the AA on one side and the dove on the other that were found at the scene of the crimes? The Caller chuckled and said, Mr. Carter, as the saying goes, I'm going to leave something for your imagination, in other words if you don't figure it out then at some point in our relationship I will reveal why they were left at the scene and what they represent. So Mr. Carter it's been interesting talking to you and if its God will I look forward to our next conversation. The caller said good night and before I had an opportunity to reciprocate I heard a dial tone in my ear.

I hung up the phone and walked over to my sofa and sat down thinking, what just happened, and what did I just commit to. I took out a notepad and made some notes about the conversation I just had with the Caller. It was now pass my bedtime even though I knew that I would probably not sleep at all tonight because of trying to process everything that was revealed to me.

The following morning, I prepared to go to work with minimum sleep hoping that none of my coworkers would question me about the information I shared with them the previous week. The last thing I need at this time is one of them snooping around me or my office and coming across information related to the Caller and our communications.

That morning during our staff meeting Stan asked each of us did we come across anything new related to the assassinations. Then Stan looked in my direction and asked did I receive any more threatening phone calls? I answered no and that I was starting to believe that the one call wasn't legitimate and that it may have been a hoax. Stan stated that nevertheless we should remain vigilant about possible dangers coming from whoever may be committing theses heinous acts.

The meeting ended and I headed to my office thinking about the lie I just told my coworkers. I hated the fact that I had to lie to them but this may be the only way to protect them and me. My back was now against the wall and the only way out was forward and make this new relationship with the Caller work and come out of this with a great front page story.

The rest of day I did some research and made some phone calls to attempt to find out if there were ever similar crimes committed in other major cities and other New York boroughs besides Manhattan.

Later that afternoon Stan call for an emergency team meeting because one of the detectives wanted to share some information regarding their investigation. hen

When I walked in to the conference room for the meeting Detective Harrison was seated at the table. Somehow

I got the impression that Detective Harrison didn't remember me from that night when Judge Barrows was murdered near my apartment building. As I sat down at the table I could tell by his stare that maybe he was starting to recall where he knew me from.

Stan open the meeting by reintroducing Detective Harrison and asking the team to give him our full attention.

Detective Harrison started by saying that the police department has sources and informants that work the streets undercover and incognito and that they take dangerous risk to help law enforcement do their jobs successfully. He went on to say that one or more of their informants has confirmed that the group responsible for these assassinations on our public officials are part of a group of twenty-five or more and that some of them have serve prison time and they have made a threat against the media and journalist who investigate them. So I came here to inform you and to warn you that as a newspaper company and as journalist you may have a bullseye on your back.

Detective Harrison gave each of us his business card and adamantly insisted that if we see or hear anything out of the ordinary that we were to contact him or other law enforcement immediately.

As Detective Harrison got up to leave I could not help but think about the five men dressed in black at the faith leaders meeting and whether the caller was one of them. As the team was leaving the conference room Stan reminded us to heed Detective Harrison's warning and to not let our guard down around strangers.

As I was walking back to my office I began to think that everything and all of the evidence so far was pointing in the direction of the Sons Of Anarchy for these assassinations. It was one thing to have a suspicion about someone but a whole different world and quite the challenge to prove it.

I spent the next few hours organizing my notes and making some phone calls to a few contacts that I haven't been in touch with for quite some time but nothing of value came out of it. I knew that somehow I had to get some solid evidence to prove who was behind these assassinations or I might be standing in the unemployment line if Stan found out I was keeping information from him.

I got up from my desk and walked over to the window and stared down at the busy New York street when someone knocked and called my name. It was my coworker Susan with news that Detective Smith had called and informed Stan that they had made an arrest related to the assassinations of the public officials. Susan also informed me that only one white male had been arrested and that the evidence that they had was at best wanting. I thanked her for sharing the information and asked her to keep me informed if and when she hears additional information related to the arrest.

The Anointed Assassin

I sat at my desk thinking about the news I just received and wondered whether the person who was arrested could possibly be the Caller. As much as I wanted the murders to end like everyone else I also hoped that the person who was arrested was not the caller because he was my inside source to a great story that would help me keep my job. It was now late in the day and close to 5 O'clock so I decided to pack it in and head home for the day hoping that when I did get home that I would hear from the Caller.

As I got on the subway heading for home there was hardly room to move, or sit, or stand, because of the rush hour crowd. I felt a feeling of paranoia thinking to myself that anyone of the individuals on this train could be a member of the group responsible or involved in the assassinations. I remembered what Stan said about not trusting strangers.

As I exited the subway station and started the three block walk to my apartment it was difficult to do so without constantly looking back over my shoulders. I finally reached my building and before pulling out my keys I took a minute to look around to make sure I wasn't being followed. I opened the door to my apartment and before walking all the way in I listened momentarily to make sure there wasn't anyone waiting inside.

I had to come to the realization and acceptance that investigating these assassinations was starting to take its toll on me emotionally and mentally.

After securing the three locks on my door, I kicked of my shoes, grabbed a beer from the refrigerator, turned on the television to the news and stretched out on the sofa. As I laid there I couldn't help but think back to what my Mom told me and my sister about choosing a profession. She would tell us that if we chose a profession that we loved and enjoyed we would never work a day in our lives. In other words, she was saying when you are doing something that you love it's not work.

I fell asleep and woke up in a cold sweat because I had dreamed that I was being chased my two men in a black SUV. I got up and headed for the bathroom and just as I started the shower the telephone rang. As I rushed out of the bathroom without turning off the shower I was hoping and praying that the call was from Caller. Just as I reached for the phone it stopped ringing but I still picked it up and said hello, but there was no answer and no message. The call made me feel a bit uneasy because I could not remember the last time if ever receiving an anonymous or a hang up phone call.

I waited a few minutes before going back in the bathroom hoping that whoever it was they would call again but the phone did not ring.

I returned to my shower, this time taking the phone into the bathroom with me. After my shower I grabbed another beer from the refrigerator and flopped down on the sofa watching the news and watching my phone hoping it would ring.

It was now after ten and I decided to go to bed thinking that maybe it was in fact Caller who was arrested since I didn't receive a phone call from him. I lied in bed fighting sleep hoping that my phone would ring and it would be the Caller. Unfortunately, tiredness and sleep got the better of me and I fell into a deep sleep. All of a I was dreaming and hearing this constant ringing in the dream. I managed to pull myself out of my stupor and realized that it was actually my cell phone that was ringing.

I looked over at my alarm clock and was surprise to see that it was well after midnight when I reached over an answered the phone. I was still groggy and half asleep when the voice on the other end of the phone said wake up Mr. Carter, I do apologize for calling at such a late hour.

Half asleep I responded that it was okay and that I was in fact happy and relieved to hear his voice because I was concerned that maybe the person who was arrested earlier today was him. The Caller chuckled and said that it was his opinion that the police made that arrest knowing they didn't have the right person. He went on to say that they did it to pacify the public out of fear of being seen that they were not doing enough to solve who is behind the assassinations.

I asked the Caller what did he know about the person who was arrested? He answered not a lot only that he could assure me that the person arrested is not a member of his group. I asked him how many members was in his group and what kind of background do they have? He chuckled and said that he was not ready to share that information and that it was going to be a real shocker when he does share the members background.

The Caller stated that the group is planning another assassination and it is supposed to take place two days from today and the target is State Senator Willie Carr. I asked the Caller what was he going to do to stop it from happening? The Caller responded, that's where you come in Mr. Carter. I asked the Caller what is it that I could do to prevent the assassination of Senator Carr without putting myself in harm's way. The Caller suggested that I send the Senator an anonymous email from a library computer or make an anonymous call from a pay phone or leave an anonymous voice mail message. I asked the caller why don't he contact the Senator himself? He answered that it was too risky and if something were to go wrong they might be able to retrace where the warning came from.

Am I My Brother's Keeper

The Caller shared that he was also concerned about his colleagues becoming aware that he is talking to a journalist and retaliate by hurting his family. I told the Caller that I wanted the assassinations to end and therefore I would consider his proposal only if he would commit to giving me an exclusive account of everything that has transpired with the group from the beginning until these cruel acts comes to an end. The Caller said that because of some unusual experiences that have been happening to him recently he wants the same and is committed to giving me details about everything they did and who they are.

I told the Caller I would do what I can to warn the senator but I was also concerned about the repercussions from my employer, law enforcement and your comrades. The Caller ask what kind of repercussions would I receive from my employer and law enforcement? I answered that I could be fired because I haven't been honest and forthright with my employer about my communications with him and law enforcement could charge me with aiding and abetting a felon in committing a crime. The Caller responded that he understood my fears and concerns and that he would do everything within his powers to safeguard and protect my name and reputation. I told the Caller thank you and that I would do the same for him.

I asked the Caller what was his plan for getting his colleagues to end theses assassinations. He answered that he hinted to them that maybe what we had done so far may have accomplished our goal of convincing public officials that they need to do a better job of serving the public. He went on to say that they questioned him about his loyalty to the goals that they had set in the beginning and if he was no longer committed to those goals he needed to let them know.

I asked Caller what was the initial goal of group? The Caller stated that the initial goal of the group was to eliminate crooked and corrupt politicians and judges and send a message that their behavior would not be tolerated at the taxpayer's expense. The Caller said, so Mr. Carter at this time I'm at lost as to how to resolve this issue with my colleagues and I'm hoping the two of us can put our heads together and come up with a plan. I responded, you want me to help you come up with a plan that could possibly put you and your associates in prison or worse both you and them could get the death penalty. The Caller responded, yes, that he knows what he is asking sounds ludicrous but he believes he is being spiritually led and somehow he would be okay. I told Caller that I would figure out a way to get a message to the senator then we both said goodnight.

I lied awake most of the night thinking about

The Anointed Assassin

Department related to the recent assassinations. I told Stan to inform Jerry and the others that I would be down to the conference room shortly after I make a bathroom stop.

The truth is, I did need to go to the bathroom but not to relieve myself but to settle my nerves and compose myself because I knew that my text to the senator was the reason for the press conference that was about to be held.

I sat in one of the stalls for a minute telling myself over and over that what I did was the right thing and if it was revealed that I sent the email I could justify my actions by the life that was saved. I rubbed my sweaty palms together and said a short prayer and came out of the stall and threw some water on my face and headed down to the conference room.

As I walked into the conference room everyone eyes was on me and I felt like everyone knew what I had done. Jerry chuckled and said thanks for joining us Mr. Carter, your just in time, the press conference is just about to start.

The voice from the television announce that they were interrupting the current program to bring you breaking news about the recent wave of assassinations of politicians and judges in the city of New York. The newscaster announce that we will now hear from Senator Willie Carr who shared with our reporter that he was warned of an assassination attempt, here is Senator Carr.

The Senator slowly walked up to the microphone and said, good afternoon fellow New Yorker, I am Senator Willie Carr and a few hours ago I received an anonymous email warning me that I had been targeted to be assassinated by the same group of individuals who assassinated four of my colleagues and made an attempt on the fifth unsuccessfully. I would like to thank the concerned citizen who sent me the email and would like to suggest that you contact the New York city police department and assist them with bringing those who are responsible to justice.

The Senator went on to say that together with his office and the mayor's office there is a Twenty-Five Thousand Dollars reward, for information leading to the arrest and conviction of those responsible. The Senator added that police Captain Henson from the third precinct had some additional information he wanted to share with the public.

Captain Henson walked up to the microphone and reiterated what Senator Carr said, and stated that the person who sent the anonymous email to the senator should come forward and identify themselves and if the information they share lead to an arrest they would be entitled to the Twenty-Five Thousand Dollars reward and would be doing a great public service. He went on to say that his department is currently doing and investigation to determine where and who the email came from in hopes of bringing the violence toward our public servants to an end.

Captain Henson made an appeal to the public stating that the police department needs the public help to solve crime and keep the city and neighborhoods safe. Captain Henson read off two toll free numbers that the public could call with tips and information including the senator's office and the mayor's office. Captain Henson stated that he would like to close the press conference by saying that once the investigation is completed about the email that there would be a follow press conference if necessary.

After the press conference ended Jerry turned the television off and added that we as investigative reporters needed to step up our game and come with some conclusive information related to these assassinations. Jerry went on to add that he has been authorized from the higher ups to offer a Thousand Dollars bonus and a paid week off to the first reporter to produce solid evidence about who is behind these atrocities that are taking place in our city.

All of sudden everyone in the room perk up and there was chatter coming from every direction and from everyone. Jerry ended the meeting and we exited the conference room and returned to our office.

As I was walking back to my office I could not help but think about the Twenty-Five Thousand Dollars reward, the Thousand Dollar bonus and the extra paid week off. Nevertheless, I had to keep my priority straight because getting the exclusive details of what transpired from the beginning until the conclusion of the assassin's mission was more important than any reward or vacation. When I returned to my office I decided I would finish the call to Dee that I started to make before we were called into the meeting.

I dialed Dee's number an after about the seventh ring she answered the phone. Before I could say a word she said, hello, Terry Carter, I was thinking about you, what's new? I responded that I have the exact same question for you, what's new? Have you come across anything new related to the assassinations? She answered well, I saw a very interesting press conference a little while ago held by Senator Carr and Police Captain Henson. I asked her what did she think about the press conference. Dee answered that she was curious about the email and who sent it, and she was highly curious and motivated by the reward offered by the senator.

Dee also stated that she hadn't heard anything new or interesting except that tomorrow night is the faith leader's monthly community meeting. I asked Dee was she planning on attending the meeting? She answered yes, she would be attending because there was something about the meetings that she finds mysterious and intriguing. I answered that I find the meeting somewhat informative but I can't say that I find them mysterious or intriguing. Dee chuckled and said maybe that's because you are from Mars and I'm from Venus. I laughed and said, is that so. She responded, yep, that was the latest intergalactic news about men and women. We both laughed and I told Dee that I would see her tomorrow night and we ended the call.

Back In The Game

Shortly after I hung up the phone after speaking with Dee my phone rang and I could see from the caller ID that it was Styx. When I said hello I could hear the excitement in Styx voice when he responded, Mr. Carter, I got your voicemail message and the only news I have for you now is that I'm back in the game. I responded, what do you mean when you say you are back in the game? Styx answered that because of what happened to Cosmos he was a bit reluctant to continue looking into information and clues about who has been taking out our so call public servants.

He went on to say that because of the press conference he saw on television earlier about the Twenty-Five Thousand Dollars reward that it has motivated him and helped him get pass all of his fears. I asked Styx, so your telling me that I can reach out to you going forward about information related to who is behind these murders of New York city judges and politicians. Styx responded, oh Yeah, I am highly motivated because twenty-five thousand dead presidents will put me right where I need to be. I asked Styx, and where is that, where is it that you think you need to be? Styx answered that him and his girlfriend want to get engage and eventually get married and move out of the city.

I asked Styx would he be attending the faith leaders meeting tomorrow night? He answered yes, that he would be there because going forward he is not passing up any opportunity to gather information because he intends to claim the reward being offered by the senator. I told Styx that I was glad that he was, as he put it, back in the game and that I look forward to working with him again and that I would see him tomorrow night and we ended the call.

Family Matters

It had been a while since I spoke to my Mom and Dad so I decided I would give them a call before leaving work to go home. I thought to myself as I dialed their number were they fully aware of the tragedies that has been occurring in the city they strongly advised me against moving to. My Mom answered the phone on the first ring and when she heard my voice she started crying. I asked my Mom what was wrong, was everything alright, is everyone okay? She answered Yes, I am just happy and excited to hear your voice. I asked my Mom how was she and how was dad? She answered that both of them were fine and that dad had gone fishing with the neighbor.

My Dad and Mom both were in their sixties and had retired about five years ago and therefore my Dad spent most his time fishing. I asked my Mom had she spoken to my sister Karen and my older brother Robert? She answered that she speaks to both of them at least once a week and she was grateful to God that they didn't live in a dangerous city like New York. I responded that New York may not be the safest city but it's an exciting city and that I am always careful and that I do remember to pray from time to time. She answered that she was glad to hear that I didn't forget that one lesson because God is the best protection you can have especially when you live in such a dangerous place.

My Mom stated that she had seen on the news where there had been several murders of judges and politicians and that makes her afraid for me. I laughed and said, well Mom, I am not a politician or a judge and I have no plans now or ever of becoming one. My Mom said she would tell dad that I called and that I needed to call more frequently and that I should reach out to my brother and sister and to be safe. I told my Mom that I promise to call more often, and that I would reach out to both my brother and sister soon, and that I would be safe, and that I would not forget to pray, and we ended the call.

Before leaving to go home I stood from my desk and looked out the fourth floor window at the always busy New York Street and wondered how did I get here and did I make the right choice. And what I mean by here is, working as an investigative journalist in an over-crowded and dangerous city on a story that had the potential to put my life in danger. I took a deep breath and exhale and told myself the infamous lie we tell ourselves when we are not sure about the choice we've made, "no guts, no glory."

As I walked out of eighty-two story building that housed the Manhattan Times on to the busy street I got this feeling in the pit of my stomach that someone was watching me and/or following me. As I walked to the Metro Station I tried not to but I kept looking over my shoulders. Once I was seated on the train I was able to let go of some of the fear of being shot or stab in the back. On the ride home I remembered what my Mom said about my decision to live in a dangerous city like New York.

Candid Camera

Once I arrived at home the first thing I did was make sure I had locked the doors and windows behind me and close the blinds tightly.

I did my usual thing when I first get home from work which is to grab a beer and turn on the news. As I sat on my sofa finally feeling a bit of relief from the stress of the day a voice on the television announce that they were interrupting the regular news to bring a special news bulletin from New York City Police Department.

Captain Henson announced that this news press conference was a follow-up from the earlier press conference concerning and email sent to Senator Carr. He stated that they were able to trace where the email was sent from and that they had film footage of a possible suspect who sent the email. On the television screen was a picture of me sitting at a computer and walking out of the library. I sat on my sofa with my heart beating so fast I thought it was coming out of my chest. Nevertheless, I was somewhat relieved when I realized that because of the poor quality of the picture it was almost impossible for anyone to recognize me.

Captain Henson went on to say that the person in the video was not guilty of a crime or anything else and the police department would appreciate it if the person in the video would come forward and assist them in their investigation. He went on to say that if anyone recognize the person in the video please contact their local police department and if this leads to an arrest and conviction of those behind the latest attacks on our politicians and judges they would be entitled to the reward being offered.

The Captain stated that he wanted to end the press conference by sending a strong message to those that are reaping havoc in our city by attacking our public servants. Captain Henson stated that this is a warning to those responsible. Captain Henson stated that "it was just a matter of time before they apprehend the perpetrators and he promised that those responsible would be prosecuted to the full extent of the law, including the death penalty if applicable, again you have been warned".

After the press conference ended I turned the television off because I needed a moment of quietness so that I could collect my thoughts. I realized that I had now cross over into the abyss and that every move from this point forward would have to be carefully thought through and as my mother would say, and prayed over. My thoughts were racing a hundred miles an hour and I was starting to doubt myself and some of my decisions so I decided this was a good time to pray and ask God for direction.

In other words, should I go to the authorities with what I know, or should I tell my co-workers what I know, or should I keep going in the direction I initially planned. As nervous as I was, or more correctly stated, scared out of my wits, I wasn't one to quit once I set a goal. I made the decision that I was going to stay the course because there is another saying besides "no guts no glory" and that is, "winners never quit, and quitters never win".

After I was able to collect myself and settle my nerves I decided to turn the television back on to the news. And to my surprise the newscaster announced that they had a second news bulletin that was coming from Senator Carr's home.

The Senator came on the screen and announce that while him and his family was away from their home someone left a package in their mailbox containing a plastic coin along with a message stating and I quote" soon or later we are going to get you and all of your colleagues who are wasting our tax dollars "end of quote.

The Senator went on to say that he wasn't going to be intimidated by a bunch of cowardly thugs who have no morals or ethics and are willing to commit stupid acts of violence like murder to accomplish a senseless goal. I could hardly believe what I was hearing and seeing on the television screen. I asked myself where the Caller was and what part has he played or is playing in the events that have transpired today.

Part 4. David vs Goliath

> "Learning to walk by faith comes one lesson at a time, one day at a time"...
> IG

The Walls Of Jericho

After work upon arriving home I normally would have a beer or two to relax and unwind but today I needed something much stronger. Fortunately, I do keep a bottle of scotch and a bottle of Jack Daniels around for my few friends who don't like beer.

After having a stiff drink of scotch and a beer I was able to steady myself and focus my thoughts on some research work I needed to get done by noon tomorrow. I had become so involved in the research work that when I finally look at the time on my laptop two hours had gone by and then my cell phone rang.

When I look over at the caller ID on my phone it showed number not available so I immediately answered it hoping it was the Caller. I hesitantly said, hello, and the voice on the other end answered Mr. Carter, I hear a lot of tension and stress in your voice, does that have anything to do with today's events. I have to admit that I was somewhat relieved when I heard the Caller's voice on the other end of the phone because I was hoping he could give me some assurance and answers about today's events.

My first question to the Caller was, is it safe, am I safe? My second question was, did you participate with your colleagues leaving the package with a coin and a threatening message at Senator's Carr's home? And before he could answer the first and second questions I rattled off a third question about how did his colleagues react to the warning Senator Carr received?

The Caller responded that the answer to my first question was that I was safe, and the answer to the second and third question was, that it was his colleague's decision to leave the package in the Senators mailbox with the coin and the threatening message. He stated that they were so angry about the fact that the Senator was warned that they were willing to risk being caught so that they could send a message to the Senator that he was not off the hook and soon if not later he was going to get served.

I asked the Caller was he certain that he had made a definite decision to disassociate himself from his colleagues and the assassinations or was he using me to further their goals. In a somewhat angry tone the Caller responded that if he was not serious about stopping the attacks then I did have something to worry about because that means Mr. Carter we would have to eliminate you. The Caller went on to say that I could relax and breathe easy because he was quite serious about his decision because of the vision and the dream that he shared with me earlier that has change his life forever.

I asked the Caller was he aware of the Faith Leaders monthly community meetings to stop the violence in the city. He answered that he was aware of their monthly meetings and stated that he did attend one of them and thought they were unproductive and a waste of time. He went on to say that the only reason these Faith Leaders are holding the meetings was to promote themselves and increase the number of their congregations and therefore increase revenue.

I told the Caller that I had attended the two previous meetings and that I would be attending the one being held tomorrow evening and suggested that he should also come. The Caller laughed and responded that he would give it some thought and if he did decide to come he would be sure to tap me on the shoulder and introduce himself.

I asked the Caller why wasn't his colleagues suspicious about how and who warned Senator Carr about the assassination attempt? He answered that they are in fact suspicious but in addition to himself there are a few other members that has express reluctance to further violence but they were easily persuaded to follow the majorities decision. The Caller told me that the group is so large that there are leaders and there are soldiers and currently they are trying to figure out who in the group betrayed the group and sent the email.

Judge, Jury, and Executioner

The Caller informed me that some of his colleagues are so determine to eradicate what they describe as institutional and government avarice that they have made a vow to give their lives if necessary to deal with these self-serving con artists.

I told the Caller that I wanted to keep working with him until this nightmare has come to its conclusion but that it was nerve racking and stressful and that he needed to find a way to expose the group and end this madness as soon as possible. The Caller responded that he agreed with me nevertheless he was the one who initially came up with the idea and therefore would feel responsible if anything happens to some of the members who are longtime friends.

I asked the Caller has there been any conversation among his colleagues about another target. The Caller responded that the group has decided that they are going to wait a few days before deciding on the next target but Senator Carr is one target that they are determine to eliminate because he is at the top of the list when it comes to greed and corruption.

I asked the Caller how did him and his colleagues go about gathering evidence that certain politicians were abusing their positions and therefore wasting the taxpayer's money and violating the public trust. The Caller responded that there were members in the group with all types of professional backgrounds including some with degrees on many levels and in various fields. So to answer your question Mr. Carter we have members in our group that have access to business, political, and personal information about every judge and politician that we have determine to be unfit to serve and has to be eliminated because of their greed.

The Caller shared that there are some individuals that are truly public servants and we commend them for their ethical and moral behavior and their integrity. The Caller stated that you never know Mr. Carter maybe some of our colleagues are politicians and therefore are supplying the group with the necessary evidence needed to determine who is corrupt and has to go. I told the Caller that it sounds as if he and his colleagues have convinced themselves that they are justified in committing murder and have made themselves judge, jury and executioner.

I asked the Caller that if he and his colleagues have solid evidence against judges and politicians that are corrupt and wasting the taxpayer's money and taking kick-backs why not go through normal channels and report them to the proper state and/or federal authorities and let the judicial system handle it. He responded that they tried that before by sending in anonymous tips with solid information but the authorities wanted them to come to court and testify publicly. The Caller stated that one of his long-time friends who had decided to testify publicly in court never made it to court.

The Caller went on to say that some of the politicians who are in office were elected because of ties to organized crime and that their campaigns were mostly financed by money that was made from illegal activities.

I asked the Caller that in addition to politicians and judges being in the pocket and under the influence organize crime did he think that there were also some police officers included in that group? The Caller responded that him and his colleagues haven't identified any yet but he would be willing to bet a hundred to one that there are some who are beholden to an individual or some type of organized crime.

The Caller informed me that their first priority is the politicians and judges but in due time the group is planning to investigate the activities of corrupt police officers who have cross the line and have taken kickbacks. I asked the Caller, of the four politicians recently assassinated in the city of New York how many of them did he actually assisted in or was the shooter?

The Caller answered that sometimes he is the driver and sometimes he was the shooter but he would prefer not to get in to specifics about who did what, when, and where at this time. I told the Caller that I have no problem respecting those wishes at this time but I needed to remind him that I decided to work with him with the stipulations that he would give me an exclusive story including the details and the specifics of everything that has happen with him and his colleagues. The Caller answered that he was a man of his word and that when the time was right he would gladly fulfill that commitment.

The Caller shared with me that going forward he will neither be the driver or the shooter because what him and his colleagues did was wrong and he wish there was a way he could take it back. I asked the Caller why won't you go to the proper authorities and ask for protection and immunity and stop this nightmare before your colleagues find out that you are the leak and eliminate you or one of your family members, and God forbid, me. The Caller answered that he thought about that but his fear is that the federal authorities will step in and take the case from the state of New York and make the death penalty mandatory. He went on to say that if there was a way he could insure that his colleagues would not be sentenced to death he would step forward and stop what has been the worst decision of his life in bringing this group together.

The Good Shepherd

All of a sudden the Caller with excitement screamed through the phone that he had a great idea. With hesitation and suspicion, I asked, and what is your great idea? He answered that why don't you go to the authorities and investigate their position by creating a scenario involving the possibility of an individual offering a peaceful surrender of himself and the group with the stipulation that none of the members would receive the death penalty. I responded that first you ask me to risk my safety by sending a warning message to Senator Carr and now you are asking me to go to the authorities and inform them that I have been communicating with the group responsible for assassinating judges and politicians?

The Caller responded that he appreciated everything I had done and understood that he was asking a lot from me but he didn't know any other way to resolve the issue at hand. I told the Caller that I would think about it and pray about it but at this point I could honestly say that the answer would probably be no to such a precarious request. The Caller responded, yes, think about it and definitely pray about it and I will be praying that you are spiritually led and protected if your decision is yes. I told the Caller that he shouldn't get his hopes up because it would take a miracle for me to say yes to do what he is asking and we both said goodnight.

It was now late in the evening so I decided to have a nightcap and turn in a bit earlier than normal. I lied there in bed looking up at the ceiling praying and thinking about everything that transpired today especially the conversation I had with the Caller about going to the to the authorities to test their position if the assassins turned themselves in. I finally dozed off and when I woke up the next morning I realized that I had dreamed that I went to the authorities on behalf of the assassins and received a positive response stating that they were willing to keep the death penalty off the table. I was baffled by the dream because I did pray about the decision to go or not to go and this dream was like a confirmation that I should in fact go.

As I was getting ready for work that morning and wrestling with the dream I realized and thought to myself that it would take more than a dream for me to move forward with this decision, in other words, it would definitely take a miracle.

As I was walking the three blocks from my

The Anointed Assassin

apartment to the subway station I had this creepy feeling that someone was watching and following me.

Before entering the Metro-Station I stop at the newsstand and bought a newspaper from Jimmy who has been working at this newsstand since I moved into the neighborhood five years ago. After I gave Jimmy the money for the paper, he commented, Mr. Carter you seemed to be out of sorts today and a bit preoccupied. I asked Jimmy what made him say that? He responded that you are fidgety and you keep looking over your shoulder and you gave me fifty dollars for the paper when you have several smaller bills in your hand. I apologize to Jimmy using for an excuse for my behavior that I didn't sleep well and it was probably the extra cup of coffee I had this morning that made me jumpy.

As I sat on the train trying to focus my mind and concentrate on the newspaper in my lap I had this strong suspicion that someone was staring at me. I looked up quickly to try to make eye contact with whoever it was that was staring and two different men on opposite sides of the train looked away quickly.

Something inside of me wanted to go over and ask them if they knew me or had I met them before but fear got the better of me and I stayed seated. When the train pulled into my stop I hesitated to get up and waited to see what the two men would do. Both of them glanced at me quickly but only one of the men stood up to get off at the same stop that I was getting off. I waited until seconds before the door was about to close before rushing and exiting the train. I stood and waited on the platform and watched to see what direction the man who exited the train was going in. I was somewhat relieved when he exited the station using a different exit from the one that I would use to get to the building where I work.

Before entering my building and going upstairs to my office I went in to the Starbucks next door to get a pastry and a coffee and as I was leaving the same man from the train was coming in to Starbucks. As we passed each other our eyes met briefly and my coffee slipped out of my hands. I am not the type of person to make a mess and leave it undone but I wanted to get as far away as possible from this person.

As I entered my building and got on the elevator with Tom he stared at me for a moment then stated that I was white as a sheet as if I had seen a ghost. I wanted to respond to Tom but it seemed as if my brain was frozen and unable to communicate with my mouth. When the elevator reached our floor and the door open I was finally able to grunt out the words that I was fine.

I went to my office and sat at my desk staring out the window down at the busy New York street to see if the man from the train was standing near my building or the Starbucks. After a few minutes of intensely scanning down at the crowd in front of my building and Starbucks I didn't see any sign of him.

As I sat at my desk with a million thoughts running through my head I wondered if the Caller's colleagues had caught wind of our communications and was now coming after me. Then a second thought came in my head that maybe it was just my imagination and the two men on the train was coincidental and it had nothing to do with me.

The Faith Leaders meeting was being held tonight and I started to feel uncomfortable about attending it alone so I decided to ask Tom or Stan if they were interested in attending. Unfortunately, both of them responded that they had other plans and asked me what was my reasoning for attending the meetings and what did I get out of them. I answered that I was informed by one of my source that there is information to be uncovered at the meetings and also there is something suspicious about the five men dressed in black that attend the meetings.

Here We Go Again

As I was walking back to my office Lisa came hurriedly down the hall stating that Jerry wanted everyone to meet in the conference room right away. When I walked into the conference room everyone from the Insight Team was there anxiously waiting for Jerry. After about five minutes Jerry finally walked in with a somber expression on his face as if he was about to break down and cry. We all knew from his facial expression and body language that something terrible had happen.

Jerry sat down at the conference table without saying anything for about sixty seconds and then finally said, it has happened again. Right away we all knew what Jerry meant when he said it has happened again. Jerry just sat there in silence with a blank stare as we anxiously waited for the details and the specifics about what happen.

Jerry finally stated that both Senator Carr and his body guard was gunned down in an underground parking garage near a strip mall outside the city. Jerry stood up and turned on the television and plastered across the screen was a news reporter standing in front of the strip mall with yellow tape and plenty of police activity in the background.

The reporter stated that both Senator Carr and his body guard were shot several times and that both were pronounced dead upon arrival at Manhattan General hospital. The reporter went on to say that it hasn't been confirmed by the police department yet but the word is that nine millimeter shell casings and a small plastic coin were recovered from the scene.

Jerry pounded his fist on the desk and asked what is it with these lunatics who believe that violence is a means to and end and what is it with theses freaking coins. Jerry went on to say that he wanted to remind us that our job in Insight as investigative reporters is to dig and search until we find the source behind the story and lately Insight has failed to represent the newspapers standards.

With and unhappy look on his face and anger in his voice Jerry asked, who sitting at this table can share something about these assassinations that I can take to my boss that would justify the Insight Department existence. There was dead silence in the room for a half of minute before I answered that the coins found today and the ones I gave you and the police is probably the way the assassins identify themselves.

Jerry responded, Terry I appreciate the coins that you gave me and the police a while back but that is old news and right now we need something new, something fresh, and something definitive to solve this mystery. I told Jerry and my coworkers that I was attending the Faith Leaders meeting tonight and that I have a gut feeling that there may be a connection of some kind or a source of information related to the meetings and I was hoping one of them would accompany me.

Everyone remained silent and finally Jerry asked, what did I gain from attending the previous two meetings and what made me think that tonight would be any different. I responded that at this time I can't put my finger on it but I truly believe there is a connection and I prefer not to go alone. Tom asked why and did it have anything to do with the way you were acting earlier in the elevator? Jerry asked, what happen in the elevator? Before I could say nothing happened Tom interrupted me and said he saw me on the elevator earlier and that I was white as a sheet like I had just seen a ghost. Jerry interjected and asked, Terry is there something you are not telling us that you need to get off of your chest.

A bit nervous and annoyed at Tom for outing me, I answered that there wasn't anything I needed to share or get off my chest, it's just that I thought that four eyes and four ears could gather information better than two.

Jerry asked my coworkers if anyone of them wanted to accompany me to the Faith Leaders meeting tonight? All of my coworkers remain silent and motionless and none of them would even make eye contact with me. Jerry responded, well Terry there you have it, I guess you are on your own and I hope that something miraculous happens tonight because God knows Insight needs to step up its game.

A Helping Hand

Jerry then went on to say that he had recently hired a reporter by the name of Rick Wentz who has ten years of investigative experience working for the West Coast Times and he will be starting on Monday. Jerry stated that Rick investigated and help convict a group of doctors who was responsible for scamming the government out of millions of dollars through fraudulent medical claims. Jerry told Tom, who is the assistant manager of Insight that he wanted him to team up with Rick and focus on finding out who is behind these assassinations.

Jerry added that just because new blood was coming on board that it didn't mean that the rest of us need to get complacent and slack up on our efforts because we need to resolve this issue as a team. Jerry dismissed the meeting and as I walked back to my office I felt guilty about not being truthful with my coworkers. I was in fact afraid, or better said, petrified of attending the Faith Leaders meeting alone because of the men on the train and because of what happen earlier to Senator Carr and his bodyguard. The only other option that I could think of to keep from going to the meeting alone was to call Dee and see if she was attending and if so ask her to meet me at Barney's.

I dialed Dee's number and when she answered I could hear a male voice in the background who sounded as if he was angry. I asked Dee if everything was okay and did she have a minute to talk? Dee responded that everything was okay and that she was dealing with an irate customer and she did have a few seconds to talk. I asked Dee if she was attending the Faith Leaders meeting tonight would she meet me at Barney's so that we could go together? Dee laughed and said sure, as long as you make it worth my while, and that she had a tidbit of information for me. I told Dee thank you and that we should meet around 5pm and we hung up.

It was some relief knowing that I wouldn't have to attend the Faith Leaders meeting tonight alone but it didn't take away enough of my fears. As I sat at my desk anticipating how to traverse my way to the meeting tonight I knew that I needed more strength and/or faith to calm this storm that was brewing in my soul. Even though I didn't consider myself to be religious or a person of faith, nevertheless, because of my emotional and mental state I decided that I would call my Mom and ask her to pray for me.

Facing Giants

I dialed my Mom's number and the phone kept ringing and ringing and finally after about ten or more rings she answered the phone. After saying hello, I asked my Mom was everything alright? She said yes she didn't answer the phone right away because she didn't recognize the number and thought it was some telemarketer trying to sell something. I apologize to my Mom and told her that my phone was set on don't show number and I had forgot to change it to show caller's number. My Mom stated, Terry I detect some kind of tension and anxiety in your voice, what is going on? I answered that a lot is going on and I'm under a lot of stress because of a story I've been working on and because of it I have had to keep some information from my coworkers. My Mom ask me to correct her if she was wrong. Did the story have anything to do with what she heard on the news today about Senator Carr and his bodyguard?

I hesitated before answering because my Mom always know when I'm being truthful so I answered yes that's why I'm calling because I need you to pray for me. My Mom answered, Terry I pray for you every day sometimes twice a day. She went on to say that what I needed to do was to surrender my life and commit my life to Jesus Christ and establish a personal relationship with Him. I answered, Mom I believe there is a God and I do pray but I don't know who he is and what his name is, that is if he has a name. She answered that I can only tell you my son that Jesus change my life and He has protected me and provided for me and if you ask Him with a sincere heart he will reveal Himself to you. I told my Mom thank you for your love and your prayers and I will think about everything she said and we said goodbye.

After hanging up the phone with my Mom I thought deeply about what she said about her faith and her relationship with Jesus Christ. While growing up I attended church with my family up until the time I started high school and after high school I drifted away from the notion of their being a God that you could know and have a personal and intimate relationship with.

Once I entered college things took a major turn because I began to believe that there wasn't any power or intelligence greater than human beings and when we die that was the end of life as we know it. Before leaving work to meet Dee at Barney's Pub I asked Stan and Tom if they may have changed their minds about attending the Faith Leaders meeting with me but both said no.

Verity And Justice

Because of my earlier experience on the train I decided that I would take a taxi to Barney's Pub to meet Dee. It was happy hour at Barney's and the pub was packed and the smoke and noise was almost unbearable. I walked to the back of the pub and there was Dee sitting at a table with a couple of guys that I had never seen before and when she saw me she got up quickly and walked towards me and we sat a couple of tables away from where they were. I asked Dee how she was and who were her friends? She answered that they were a couple of guys she met hanging out at Barney's and that I had nothing to worry about because they were harmless. I thought to myself that maybe the experience with the two men on the train earlier today was making me paranoid.

Dee stated that before we leave for the Faith Leaders meeting she wanted to have a beer and share some information with me about a certain politician who possibly may become a target. I waited until Dee had ordered her beer and the waitress delivered it before asking Dee what was the name of the politician and what information did she have about him. She answered that she wanted to make it clear that she expected to receive a healthy finder's fee for the information she was about to share because it was directly related to the recent incidents that have taken place in the city. I asked Dee, when you refer to healthy finder's fee what amount are you talking about? She answered that she expected at least three hundred dollars because the information she has clearly shows the connection between organized crime and politicians who are making decisions that assist their crooked friends and their illegal enterprises. I told Dee that if the information she has is as good as she said it was I would have no problem giving her three hundred dollars.

Dee pulled out a white envelope and took out a carbon copy of a check for two hundred and fifty thousand dollars that was made out to City Councilman Harry Jackson from a well-known mobster by the name of Lucky Moretti. I couldn't believe what I was staring at on the table and so I immediately looked around the pub to see if anyone else was looking in our direction.

My first question to Dee was where did you get this and is this an authentic copy of a real check. Dee answered that the check was as real as the nose on my face and that she has a friend that works at a local bank. I told Dee that I was willing to give her the three hundred dollars provided I could have the carbon copy of the check, and if information wasn't authentic that would be the end our relationship. Dee answered that I had nothing to worry about that this was an authentic copy of a real check and after finishing her beer we left the pub and took a taxi to the Faith Leaders meeting.

While we were in the taxi on our way to the Faith Leaders meeting Dee stated that she was curious as to why I called and ask that we attend the Faith Leaders meeting together? I hesitated for a minute before answering because I didn't want Dee to know that I was afraid and paranoid about the thought that someone was following me. I an-

The Anointed Assassin

swered that I could tell from the first time we met at the Faith Leaders meeting that she seemed familiar and comfortable in that setting and therefore could help me to navigate the meeting and gather information.

I chuckled and said that I also had a premonition that you had something special just for me. Dee laughed and answered, so not only are you a journalist, you are also a psychic. We both laughed including the cab driver as we arrived at the location where the Faith Leaders meeting was being held.

Because we arrived at the meeting a few minutes early we were able to work our way near the front and obtain seats on the second row. The four Faith Leaders were seated on the stage with two guest waiting for the crowd of about two hundred to settle down and find seats. After most of the crowd was seated Pastor John Hammond walk up to the podium and thank everyone for sacrificing their time to come out and support efforts to safeguard their communities. He went on to say that each of the Faith Leaders would share first then our two guest speakers from the city council, Councilwoman Cherie Brown, and Councilman Harry Jackson will share last and then we will have a Q&A session at the end. When I heard that one of the speakers was Councilman Harry Jackson I almost fell out of my seat.

After the Faith Leaders and Council-

153

woman Brown had spoken, Councilman Jackson approached the podium and you could hear boos coming from the rear of the room. Councilman Jackson began speaking about the need for public servants to work hard for the taxpayers while maintaining a high level of integrity, and that at the end of his current term he was going to run for mayor, and as mayor he promised to bring positive change to the city. After adding a lot of rhetoric and mumbo jumbo to try to dazzle the crowd he thanked them for coming and sat down.

Rabbi Belenky walked up to the podium and thanked everyone for coming and told the crowd that the meeting was now open for questions, and the questions could be directed to anyone on the stage. I sat contemplating for a moment and allowed other individuals to ask questions before raising my hand and stating that my question was for Councilman Jackson. I stood up to ask the councilman about his relationship with a known mobster Lucky Moretti but the words that came out was, do you take checks for political donation? Councilman Jackson answered, of course we take checks, cash, cars and of course your time as a campaign volunteer, just make sure the check is good. Everyone laughed, including the Faith Leaders and Dee, and I sat down feeling a bit embarrassed.

I immediately raised my hand again and asked the Councilman did he receive a check from a well-known mobster by the name of Lucky Moretti for two hundred and fifty thousand dollars? There was a hush that went over the entire room and if looks could kill I would be dead five times over from the looks I got from the four Faith Leaders and Councilman Jackson.

In a growling tone Councilman Jackson asked who I was? I answered that my name was Terry Carter and that I was a journalist in the Insight Department of the Manhattan Times. The councilman answered that he has received campaign contributions from many donors and that he doesn't do background checks on every donor and if I wanted to confirm whether Lucky Moretti wrote me a check for two hundred and fifty thousand dollars that maybe I should go and ask Mr. Moretti.

There was dead silence in the room for almost a minute before Imam Abdullah approach the podium and stated that they would take one more question before ending the meeting.

Dee leaned over on my shoulders and whispered in my ear, oh oh you've done it now. I knew immediately what she meant because for the most part I had just accused Councilman Jackson of being crooked and in the pocket of well-known members of organized crime. As Dee and I left the meeting she reminded me that we lived in different parts of the city and sharing a taxi home wouldn't work. I told Dee I agreed and thanked her for meeting me and the information about the check and we said goodnight.

As I sat in the back of the taxi I tried my best to relax and take my mind off of what happen today on the train and what Councilman Jackson said about asking Lucky Moretti whether he gave him a check for two hundred and fifty thousand dollars. I thought to myself maybe he was intentionally trying to instill fear in me or maybe he actually meant what he said.

When I walked through the door of my apartment I felt as if I was stepping out of the twilight zone into a world where I was now safe and I could feel a load of stress fall from my body. I went through my usual routine of getting a beer from the refrigerator and relaxing on my sofa when my cell phone rang. Before I answered the phone my instinct told me it was the Caller and I was right.

Angels And Demons

He responded, hello Mr. Carter, how was your day, uneventful I hope. I responded that my day was both eventful and stressful because on my way to work I had this sneaking suspicion that I was being followed. The Caller responded, maybe you were being followed. I blurted out, what do you mean, why would someone follow me?

The Caller stated that I had put myself in the crosshairs that drew attention to myself simply because I was investigating a very sensitive and dangerous matter related to assassinations. I asked the Caller that to his knowledge was I in any kind of danger. He answered that for the most part I had nothing to worry about at this time but I needed to be careful and tread lightly when approaching individuals whose character is suspect. I responded to the Caller that I didn't understand what he meant about approaching individuals whose character is suspect. The Caller stated that He was at the Faith Leaders meeting when I asked Councilman Jackson about receiving a check from Lucky Moretti.

The Caller asked me who was the pretty brunette sitting next to me? I didn't want the Caller to know that my relationship with Dee was that she was a source and specifically that I got the information about the check from her so I answered that she was just someone I met at the meeting.

The Caller went on to say that what I learned today about politicians like Councilman Jackson was evidence of why the group he was part do what they do by eliminating these predatory politicians. The Caller added that because of the dream and vision he had he made a vow not to commit murder ever again and he was not present when Senator Carr and his bodyguard was killed. I asked the Caller how did he manage to get out of not participating in what happened to Senator Carr. He stated that he told the group he had a family emergency out of town but he thinks they didn't buy it and suspect him of not being fully committed any longer.

I asked the Caller what was his plans to protect himself and his family if and when his colleagues become aware of his position? He answered that he was fortunate because most of his family lived in other states and he never discussed their names and where they lived with the group. I asked the Caller does his colleagues know about Councilman Jackson and his relationship with Lucky Moretti? He answered thanks to me they do now and I wouldn't want to be in Councilman Jackson shoes. I asked the Caller, so what your saying is that I could become responsible for what may happen to Councilman Jackson? The Caller answered no, Councilman Jackson is responsible for what happens to him because of his greed, in other words he should not of taken money from known crooks and gangsters.

He went on to say that all I did was my job which is investigating individuals, companies and corporations that think they can operate above the law by getting involved with misfits. What the Caller said was true yet I didn't want to be indirectly responsible for someone death even if they were corrupt and had broken the law. I asked the Caller if he thought that I should consider warning Councilman Jackson in the same way that I warned Senator Carr. The Caller responded that I needed to be careful and use discretion because his colleagues are unforgiving and I wouldn't want them as an enemy. I asked the Caller was he saying that I should do nothing and let the chips fall where they may. He responded that that was exactly what he was referring to.

He reminded me that people who try to break up fights usually are the ones who get hurt or killed so you have to know when to stay out of other people's affairs. I told the Caller that he was probably right because the risk I took in warning Senator Carr didn't reap dividends and change the outcome.

The Caller asked had I given any thought to the idea that we discussed about asking the District Attorney to take the death penalty off the table if the members of his group surrender themselves? I responded that I took a risk warning Senator Carr and as the saying goes, hind sight is twenty-twenty, and looking back I think I made a mistake doing so and I don't think your idea is a good one.

I asked the Caller what made him change his mind about introducing himself to me at the Faith Leaders meeting? The Caller stated that he thought about it but realized that doing so publicly could potentially put me in harm's way because some of his colleagues was present at the meeting.

Isaac Gavin

Faith Or Fiction

The Caller asked, Mr. Carte,r what is your opinion, or should I say, what do you believe about the existence of God, or said another way, the existence of a creator? Before I could respond the Caller asked if I was leaning in the direction of Charles Darwin's evolutionist theory, the big bang theor,y or a Creator who made man in His image? I hesitated a few seconds before responding that in high school I believed what my parents believed, and in college I leaned toward evolution, and now I'm not sure about any of it. I told the Caller I guess you could say I'm seeking and searching. The Caller responded, wow, sounds like you are a bit lost and possibly confused, but nevertheless, there is always hope and light at the end of every tunnel.

I asked the Caller what was his position on faith and God? He stated that his family was devoted to the Muslim religion and he didn't have a choice in the matter growing up but a recent revelation has change his faith to that of Christian. I asked the Caller was the catalyst that bought about this dramatic change in his religious outlook the dream and the vision that he told me about. He answered yes, and that if I was to ask Jesus with a sincere heart to reveal Himself to me that He would do so. I answered that I can't believe it's that simple. The Caller responded that as hardest as it is to believe, it is that simple.

I ask the Caller to let's change the subject to something else because the conversation about God was starting to make me feel a little uncomfortable. The Caller stated, Mr. Carter before honoring your request to change the subject of our conversation I would like to add something that may help you with your decision to ask Jesus Christ into to your life. If it wasn't for the dream, the vision, and the revelation of Jesus Christ I would still be committed to the group and to eliminating crooked dirty politicians. Mr. Carter, Jesus and His Word teach His followers to love and forgive their enemies, and from where I previously stood that's a total one eighty. Just some food for thought Mr. Carter. I told the Caller that faith in God has been a meal that I have always had difficulty swallowing and digesting.

I informed the Caller that as much as I am intrigued by our conversations and his convictions I have been consumed with a burning desire to have a face to face meeting with him. The Caller responded that he could sympathize with where I was coming from because he knew what I look like, where I worked, and where I lived. The Caller went on to say that he would pray about my request to have a face to face and that he was confident that it would happen sometime in the near future. I told the Caller that I look forward to that day and we said goodnight.

Isaac Gavin

Here Comes The Pain

The following morning shortly after arriving at work my telephone rang and when I answered, a deep growling and angry voice on the other end asked was this Terry Carter? I hesitated before asking the caller who wants to know? The voice on the other end of the phone asked, do you always answer a question with a question. This is Lucky Moretti and once again, is this Terry Carter? I have to admit I almost blanked in my pants before answering yes, how can I help you?

Mr. Moretti stated that he heard from a very reliable source that his name was the subject of a discussion about money at a community meeting last night. I responded that I also received information from a very reliable source that you gave a large sum of money to a certain councilman. Mr. Moretti responded, so what if I did, what business is that of yours. I responded that as an investigative journalist my job is to investigate activities that involved corruption and violations of public trust.

Mr. Moretti stated that he respected the fact that I have a job to do but he would suggest that going forward that I stay clear of any conversation involving his name, and if I had any questions about his finances that I should ask him dir-

The Anointed Assassin

ectly. I told Mr. Moretti that I did have a question about his finances. I asked him how did he earn his money and did he have a criminal record? The next sound I heard was a dial tone.

I hung up the telephone and leaned back in my chair thinking to myself, what hornet's nest have I just stirred? Before I could settle my nerves the telephone rang again. I wasn't sure if I wanted to answer it so I let it ring several more times before picking it up. I assume it was Mr. Moretti calling back to give me another piece of his mind but it was Councilman Jackson who asked, is this Terry Carter? I thought to myself, here we go again, I asked who wants to know? The voice on the other end responded,

Mr. Carter this is Councilman Jackson. I answered, how can I be of assistance Councilman Jackson? The Councilman stated that he was surprised and caught off guard by my question about receiving money from Lucky Moretti. I told the Councilman that it wasn't my intention to make him look bad that I was just doing my job by following up on a lead about possible government corruption. Councilman Jackson responded that I was barking up the wrong tree and that every dollar he receives from his constituents is done legally by the book.

I asked the Councilman was he aware that Lucky Moretti is known for having ties to organize crime? Councilman Jackson responded by asking me where did I get the information from about Mr. Moretti being tied to organize crime? I answered that as an investigative journalist I had my sources and that I wasn't at liberty to disclose that information. The Councilman stated that it might be a good idea if I make sure my sources were reliable before spreading rumors that could destroy a person's reputation. I told the Councilman thank you for the advice and that I would take it into consideration and that he should be careful who he does business with, especially doing business with known gangsters. The Councilman screamed, who the hell did I think I was and if I wasn't careful I could end up in the unemployment line and the next thing I heard was a dial tone.

I sat at my desk thinking to myself that I had hit the trifecta, or said another way, encountered the perfect storm, three storms colliding at the right place and the right and/or wrong time.

First I have someone who is the founder of a group that assassinates politicians and judges calling me anonymously that knows where I live and work, and what I look like. Second I have well a known member of organize crime telling me to keep his name out of my conversations. And third I have a City Councilman screaming at me and threatening to place me among the unemployed.

Part 5. Exodus

"You may not be able to do everything or help everyone, but you can do something and help someone"...IG

It's A Wonderful Life

For some unknown reason I started thinking about our purpose for being here on this planet and all I could come up with was that we human beings were vain and consumed with self-preservation. I laid my head on my desk hoping to release the depression and anxiety that was building up in my soul when all of a sudden the fire alarm started blaring. When I lifted my head from my desk Stan was standing in my door saying that there was a bomb threat and everyone needed to evacuate the building immediately.

I thought to myself as I entered the packed stairwell that in my five years of working in this building there has never been a bomb threat. I couldn't help but think that maybe this was a result of my communications with either Lucky Moretti, or Councilman Jackson, or both.

Everyone from the Insight Department huddle together on the sidewalk as several firemen entered the building to investigate whether the threat was real or a hoax. Jerry stated that more than likely one of our two thousand coworkers is probably ticked off at their husband or wife and this was their way of getting even. Everyone laughed except me. Lisa looked over at me and said, Terry, where is your sense of humor, that was funny and she started laughing hilariously. Little did she know that I was that coworker and it was not my wife that I ticked off but it was a notorious well known mobster and a Councilman.

After about thirty minutes the last of the firemen exited the building and gave the all clear so that everyone could re-enter the building. I returned to my office wondering whether it was time to lay all my cards on the table and inform Jerry and my coworkers about my communications with Caller. Also there was this friction that was now developing between myself and Lucky Moretti and Councilman Jackson and the potential for it to produce violence against myself and my coworkers. I thought to myself that maybe the best way to eliminate that potential threat is to have Caller and his colleagues eliminate the threat posed by Lucky Moretti and Councilman Jackson. As I gave the idea more thought I realized that I would be facilitating and complicit in a murder and therefore I would have blood on my hands.

Let Your Conscious Be Your Guide

Motivated by both my Mom's faith and the Caller's faith I decided to pray and ask for direction about whether I should share some of what I have uncovered with Jerry. After a brief moment of praying to my amazement I got this impression in my spirit to go forward with discussing a minimum amount of information with Jerry.

I got up from my desk and headed towards Jerry's office and twice I stopped and almost turned back. I leaned my head into Jerry's office and tapped on his door to get his attention. Jerry looked up and waved me in and pointed for me to have a seat while he finished his telephone call.

Jerry hung up his telephone, and with a kind of exasperated look on his face asked me how was my day going and how could he be service? I asked Jerry would it be okay if I closed the door to his office so that we could have some privacy? Jerry answered that it was okay to close the door and stated, "I hope I'm ready for what you're about to lay on me". I answered that it wasn't anything bad only that I had come across some inside information related to the recent assassinations of the politicians. Jerry's eyes pop open wide as he sat up straight in his chair and ask what kind of inside information are we talking about. I informed Jerry that before I share the information I need him to agree to keep this strictly between the two of us for now until certain issues have been resolved. Jerry responded that he wasn't sure he could agree to my terms until he heard more about what the information pertain to.

I informed Jerry that I was contacted by one of the founding members of the group doing the assassinations who promised to give me and our newspaper and exclusive story provided I assist him in finding a way to end the group's actions without any of them facing the death penalty. Jerry asked me how long have I been communicating with this person and how do we contact each other. I told Jerry that I refer to him as Caller and somehow he got a hold of my cell phone number and has been calling me from an anonymous phone number for the last two months. Jerry asked me what makes me believe that I can trust him and that he will keep his word. I told Jerry that he was the one responsible for warning Senator Carr, and he also shared with me that he had a dream and a vision about Jesus that changed his life forever.

Jerry asked, if this person has truly change why won't he turn himself and the members of his group to the proper authority so that these atrocities can stop. I told Jerry that it wasn't that simple because the Caller feels responsible for what happens to his friends because the initial idea to form the group was his and he is afraid they would have to face the death penalty.

Jerry leaned back in his chair and stated that I was asking a lot from him especially if there were

The Anointed Assassin

other assassinations committed in the future. I responded that I knew that I was asking a lot of him but something in my gut tells me that the Caller is going to deliver and bring these evil acts to an end.

I reminded Jerry that we were in competition with other media who were also trying to get the inside track on this story and right now we had the advantage because the Caller promised to give me an exclusive with specific details of everything that has transpired since the founding of the group.

Jerry took his glasses off and sat them on his desk and looked me in the eyes and said that he was willing to agree to what I asked but I had one month to get the goods on this story and if there were any more assassinations he would be obligated to go to the authorities and tell them what he knows. I reached over Jerry's desk and shook his hand and thanked him for believing in me and giving me the opportunity to produce what could turn out to be one of the top front page stories of the year if not the century.

I left Jerry's office feeling a hundred pounds lighter and more at ease because I no longer felt alone in this knowledge I had about an assassin and his motives for wanting to eliminate what he referred to as crooked and greedy politicians.

The Untouchables

As soon as I sat down at my desk my telephone rang and when I answered it Styx said Good morning Mr. Carter, I have some interesting news to share with you. I asked Styx was he comfortable sharing the information over the phone or was it information that needed to be shared privately face to face? Styx responded that he would rather meet at Barney's Pub and share the information with me in a face to face meeting. I told Styx that I had to make a few more calls and write a report and I would be leaving work around 4pm and I could meet him at Barney' around 4:30pm. Styx respond that he would see me then and reminded me not to forget to stop by a ATM machine because the information he had could save a life.

Just as I was getting up from my seat to leave the office to meet Styx Jerry poke his head in my office and stated with some doubt in his voice that he hoped that he had made the right decision. As I walked pass Jerry toward the elevator I responded that I know that things will work out and he didn't need to worry himself.

When I walked into Barney's the Pub was packed with the 4pm-7pm happy hour crowd. I knew Styx would be sitting somewhere near the back of the Pub facing the door. As soon as He saw me he perked up because he knew that if his information was solid he would be leaving Barney's richer than when he came in. After we said are hellos Styx stated that good news travel fast but bad news travels twice as fast. I asked Styx what was the good and/or bad news that he wanted to share with me? Styx stated that he didn't know what I had done to irritate them but there were a few people not happy with me and some comments that I made and the word on the street is that you have to be taught a lesson about sticking your nose in places where it doesn't belong.

I asked Styx what did he know about Lucky Moretti? Styx eyes popped wide open as he reared back in his chair and said, you've got to be kidding, right. I told Styx that I understand that he is affiliated with organized crime and the word is that he is a well-known member of the mafia. Styx responded that not only is he a member of the mafia and a organize crime figure he is also a made-man. I asked Styx what did it mean to be a made-man in the mafia? He responded that first of all a made-man in the mafia means he has worked his way up the ranks where he is like a general in the army. And second, no one can touch him without getting permission from the Don.

I asked Styx what does it mean to be a Don in the mafia? Styx chuckled and stated, that is another term for Godfather, or simply said another way, the head of the mafia.

Styx went on to say that all major decision go through the Godfather, especially the decision to take someone out. I told Styx that I understood what he meant when he said to take some one out. Styx hesitantly asked, is Lucky Moretti the person that you pissed off and made the comments about? I pretended I didn't hear him and went on to asked him had he heard any more about who was behind the assassinations of our politicians? Styx responded that maybe I shouldn't be concerned about politicians right now but make sure that I watch my back.

I told Styx that I would be fine, that this is what I do, I investigate people and situations, and sometimes when I do what I do, I ruffle some feathers. Styx smiled and said, well alright tough guy, I hope you know what you are doing and who you are dealing with, those people don't play fair. I gave Styx two hundred dollars and thanked him for information I already knew except for the part about certain individuals wanting to teach me a lesson about minding my business.

On the taxi ride home I thought about what kind of plans did these individuals have in mind to teach me this lesson. It was good to be home and relax with a beer and kick back on my recliner.

Before I left Indiana for New York five years ago my mother gave me a bible as a gift with these words inscribe in the inside cover, "Trust and obey Him and all will be well", Mom. As I sat holding an empty beer bottle in my hand I thought about those words and the fact that I never picked up that bible since arriving in New York. I thought about what the Caller said about asking God with sincerity to reveal Himself and He would do so.

There were a lot of different scenarios playing out in my life while investigating this story about the assassinations and I started to feel boxed end and afraid and I didn't like that feeling. I thought maybe there was something to this faith in God that I was missing but it was difficult for me to get pass my skepticism so rather than going into my bedroom and getting the bible from my closet I went to the refrigerator and took out another beer.

As I sat in my recliner looking up at the ceiling I wondered if I made the right decision becoming a journalist or if I should of followed in my father and older brothers footsteps and become a doctor. One thing I knew for sure doctors may save lives but being an investigative reporter also had the potential to save lives, tax dollars, reputations, etc., and it wasn't as boring as being a doctor. I thought about it for a minute and came to the conclusion that it is what it is and I refused to allow myself to get depressed over my career choice.

I had a lot on my plate and a lot riding on a promise that was made by someone I never met and someone who had once committed heinous crimes and now swears that he is a changed person. I was anxiously hoping that the telephone would ring because I had one month to wrap this story up and I had a unique question for Caller about a subject that baffle me. I thought to myself that maybe this was a great opportunity to see if prayer works by praying for the Caller to call. I said to myself, why not, I have nothing to lose, so I closed my eyes began to pray softly and to my surprise before I finished praying the telephone rang. When I answered it I was relieved to hear the Caller's voice say good evening Mr. Carter, you have been a naughty boy.

I responded that I was grateful that he called and I asked, what did he mean by the statement that I was a naughty boy? The Caller stated that the word around town is that you made some negatives comments about some very important and dangerous individuals. I answered that I assume that you are referring to Lucky Moretti. The Caller chuckled and stated that he was also referring to Councilman Jackson who has a reputation for dealing shrewdly with words and action towards those he considered his enemy. I told the Caller that if I allowed myself to be easily intimidated that I would not be a very effective journalist. The Caller chuckled again and stated that he understands my position but that in addition to being and effective journalist that I should want to be a living and breathing journalist. I told the Caller that I don't believe that Mr. Moretti or Councilman Jackson would go that far as to threaten my life over a news story. The Caller answered that he hoped that I was right.

I told the Caller that I had a question for him regarding how his colleagues went about choosing who met their criteria for being eliminated. I told him that the reason that I was asking that question was because I noticed that of all the assassinations that have taken place that none of them were women, why? The Caller responded that him and his colleagues made the decision not to include women as targets for elimination because God made man in his image and man should be held accountable for all the evil acts in the world not women. I asked the Caller if that decision was made because him and his colleagues are religious or was it because you see women as not being equal to men. The Caller responded that him and his colleagues see women as equal to men in some respects but we see them as the weaker vessel that men should love and protect.

The Court Of Public Opinion

I asked the Caller how would he feel if I shared our conversations with my department manager? The Caller responded that he wasn't sure if that was a good idea because if it gets back to his colleagues there could be a backlash. The Caller asked what was my motivation for wanting to share our conversations with my department manager? I answered that I feel more at ease with the knowledge that someone I trust shares the burden of knowing what I know. And secondly, I was hoping to get your consent to write an impartial story about politicians that abuse their power and how it affects the public.

I went on to tell Caller that my goal was to have the actions and behavior of these judges and politicians evaluated in the court of public opinion to assess whether they agree with the steps him and his colleagues have taken to deal with the issue.

The Caller stated that I had his consent to write a story about corruption among politicians and judges as long as I didn't allow myself to cower and be intimidated by the powers that be. I told the Caller I was aware of what I was getting into when I chose this career path so I plan to write the truth unequivocally regardless of who is affected by it. The Caller stated that he would like to remind me to be careful not to write anything specific to our conversations. I answered that I would not make that mistake and thanked him for giving me his consent to write the article and we said goodnight.

The following day when I arrived at work the first thing I did was go to Jerry's office and speak with him about the idea to write the article. After explaining to Jerry why I wanted to write the article and what I hope to gain by doing so Jerry sat quietly for a couple of minutes as if he had doubts about the idea. When Jerry finally spoke he asked, so you want to write a story about the politicians of New York city outlining some specific past and current allegations of misconduct to see what the public reaction is and to see if their position is in agreement with the assassins. I explained to Jerry that the story will not mention the actions of the assassins but will include a toll free number for them to call and voice their feelings about what discipline or punishment is appropriate to address the politician's reckless behavior. Jerry stated that he guessed it would be okay to write the article provided that it is factual and impartial and there is nothing in it that would suggest that the actions of these assassins is justified. I assured Jerry that I would follow those guidelines and told him I would like him to edit the story before it is printed.

It took a few days of researching court records and looking through old articles from other newspapers as well as our own records to get enough substance to write the story. Jerry allowed me to hire two temps to handle the feedback from incoming calls related to the story. For one week the calls never let up with the majority of callers wanting the politicians who were guilty of corruptions to serve jail time with a few exceptions who thought they should receive the death penalty.

After two weeks the temps had handle more than seven hundred incoming calls in response to the article about crooked and corrupt politicians and judges. After doing and analysis of the calls I found myself empathizing with the position of the assassins even though I believed that taking someone's life was taking it to far.

I could hardly wait until my next conversation with Caller to let him know that some of the public responses from the article agreed with the actions that him and his colleagues took to deal with the issues surrounding corrupt politicians.

I also wanted to inform Caller that he needed to find a solution that would finally terminate these assassinations and allow me to write about everything that transpired from the beginning.

It has been approximately five months since that unforgettable night near my apartment when I heard those popping sounds followed by screams coming from an underground garage.

Even though I had given Jerry and the police one of the coins with the letters AA on one side and a dove on the other, I still had one that I had kept for myself. I'm not sure exactly why I kept one of the coins but it was a tangible object that made this nightmare in New York real.

Now You Hear Me, Now You Don't

Every night for the past week I went straight

The Anointed Assassin

home from work hoping the telephone would ring and it would be Caller, but no calls. After two weeks I started to think the worse, that maybe Caller's colleagues found out about our communications and they eliminated him.

It was Tuesday afternoon of the Faith Leaders meeting when my cell phone rang and the voice on the phone said good evening Mr. Carter, I hope that I didn't worry you by not calling you in a while. I responded, yes, I was worried and that I feared the worst had happened. The Caller apologized for not calling like I had gotten accustom to him doing but stated that he had been busy working out the logistics to dissolve the group of assassins. I asked the Caller how was he planning to make that happen? The Caller stated that he was about to go on an extended trip and that I would be getting a package through FedEx in the next day or two with all the details I would need to write a powerful story about why they did what we did and why they chose the targets that they did.

I asked the Caller where was he traveling to and when would he be returning from his trip. The Caller responded that he was boarding a flight to Venezuela in thirty minutes to do missionary and evangelistic work and he was not sure when he would be returning.

I asked the Caller would it be okay if I asked him what his real name was. The Caller responded that he had recently experience a new birth and no longer cared to use his old name and stated that he liked the new name Paul because he hoped that maybe he could follow in the footsteps of Apostle Paul and make a positive and lasting difference in the world.

I thanked the Caller for keeping his word to give me the exclusive details about everything that had taken place with his group from the beginning until now and asked him to keep in touch with me from time to time. The Caller, or should I say Paul, stated that he enjoyed our conversations and he hoped that the Faith Leaders meeting tonight will be informative and insightful.

It was something in the Caller's voice that gave me the impression that this was our last conversation. I am not sure exactly what motions the Caller had put in play that would dissolve the group of assassins but I was overjoyed that this chapter in my journalistic life was coming to a close.

The thought came to my mind to give Dee a call to see if she wanted to share a taxi to the Faith Leaders meeting. The truth be told it was more than sharing a taxi that I was hoping for, it was needing to feel safe by just having another person around. Somehow I mustard up courage and decided to go alone, and on the ride to the Faith Leaders meeting I was consumed with thoughts about what the identity of the assassins would be once I received the Fed-Ex package with the an-

The Anointed Assassin

swers.

Was it the information Cosmos supplied about the Sons of Anarchy, or was it the information that Streetwise offered about a group calling themselves World Changers.

As my taxicab approach the location where the meeting was being held there was an unusual amount of traffic and I could tell that there were both marked and unmarked police cruisers.

As I approach the entrance to the auditorium there were some people mulling around on the outside and upon entering I could tell from the atmosphere that something was off. There was the normal size crowd of New York residents at the meeting and there was an abundance of police officers on both side of the stage and Captain Henson was standing at the podium, but there was no sign of the four Faith Leaders.

Come Out Come Out, Where Ever You Are

Captain Henson asked for everyone's attention and stated that he had some disturbing news to share with the audience. Captain Henson stated that the Faith Leaders are not here and he had no knowledge of their whereabouts and that they were wanted for questioning related to the assassinations of New York City politicians and judges. All of a sudden there was this unified gasp from the crowd in the room and a lot of mumbling and conversations going on at the same time.

Captain Henson asked for everyone attention again and stated that the Faith Leaders haven't been accused of any crime only that they are missing and they wanted to speak with them as soon as possible. Captain Henson went on to say that if anyone has any knowledge of the whereabouts of the Faith Leaders to please come forward and speak with one of his officers or himself.

I looked across the room and there was Dee with a cryptic smile on her face as if she wasn't surprise by the announcement. I made my way over to the area where Dee was sitting and asked her what did she make of the announcement by Captain Henson. Dee smiled and stated that maybe the Faith Leaders are not here because either they were also assassinated or maybe they are the assassins. I answered, no way these men of faith could perpetrate such a crime that involves murder.

Dee laughed and said, stranger things have happened with so call religious men like Jim Jones and others. I told Dee there has to be another explanation for the absence of the Faith Leaders. After waiting for an hour for the Faith Leaders to show up Dee and I decide to leave and we went our separate ways.

Puzzled and bewildered at home I found myself sitting in my recliner with a beer trying to wrap my head around what happen earlier today and tonight. I sat perplexed and somewhat confused asking myself whether the Caller could possibly have been one of the Faith Leaders and if so which one?

If it turned out to be true that the group responsible for these assassinations were in fact The Faith Leader's this would be one of the worse atrocities I've ever known up close perpetrated jointly by men of different faith.

I turned the television on to the news and the newscaster was reporting the news standing in front of the auditorium where the Faith Leaders meeting were held saying that the police has put out an all-points bulletin seeking the whereabouts of the four Faith Leaders.

I decided that tonight I would have something a little different than my usual beer because with everything going on in my head I knew it would be difficult for me to fall asleep. Also I decided that maybe it was time for me to investigate what was in that Bible that was hidden in my closet for the past five years to see if my Mom and Caller had in fact discovered something real and life giving. I decided that I would start by reading the Psalms and the Gospel of John and the next thing I remembered was that I was awaken the following morning by my alarm.

I could hardly wait to get to work hoping that the FedEx package would arrive today as oppose to tomorrow. When I arrived at work the first thing I did was go to Jerry's office to share the good news about the FedEx package and the bad news that he probably already knew about the

Faith Leaders dilemma. When I told Jerry about the Fed-ex package and its potential contents he reminded me that it was important that He review the information and approved the story that I hoped to write before it could be published.

I left Jerry's office excited that I was on the verge of writing a front page story that could elevate my career to the next level. When I walked into my office I felt like my heart skipped a beat when I saw the brown envelope sitting on my desk.

Before I opened the envelope I closed my office door so that I could have some privacy. When I open the envelope the first thing that fell out of it was a plastic coin like the ones that were found at the crime scene of all six assassinations. The second thing I noticed was a letter from the Caller thanking me for being patient with him and trusting him through this horrific and appalling ordeal.

The Caller stated that when I write the story about them he wanted me to include an apology to the public for their actions. The Caller added that once the public becomes fully aware of the depravity of these men's crimes hopefully they will be able to sympathize and empathize with their decisions and their actions.

In the envelope were six pages with the name of each of the individuals that was assassinated at the top with specific information about the crimes they committed. I did a quick glance through each of the six pages and was blown away when I saw the ugliness and how repulsive their crimes were.

I looked at the page with Judge Barrows name and it stated that he had on several occasion had been seen coming out of a hotel with young girls between the ages of thirteen and seventeen for the past three years.

Next I looked at the page with Councilman Harry Ford's name and it outlined several construction companies that he had receive contract kickbacks from totaling over a half million dollars.

The page with State Representative Sam Harden had pictures attached showing his brother bringing prostitutes to his condominium while the senator was visiting him.

The page with Congressman Steve Willis had a list of family members that were receiving pay checks for work they never performed.

The page with City Councilman Fred Greene had pictures of his wife after he had beaten her and convinced the police department to cover it up.

And finally Senator Willie Carr had push for a known member of organized crime to receive a casino license knowing that he made his money selling the popular and deadly narcotics fentanyl and heroin.

The worse aspect of what these judges and politicians had done was that all six of them were members of a secret underground group that exchange nude photos of young girls. After I finish reading all of the information I felt sick to my stomach and I wanted to find the remaining members of this underground group of depraved sick men and assassinate them myself.

I went to Jerry's office and shared the contents of the package with him and Jerry did what I almost did, he vomited. After Jerry pulled himself together he stated that these men are supposed to be public servants but the only person they were serving was their sick perverse appetites.

Jerry gave me the approval to write the article about the politicians and their dirty inhumane actions and why the assassins chose them to be eliminated. Jerry also stated that an article highlighting the behavior of these men may ruffle some feathers and embarrass their families but let the chips fall where they may.

After the Insight Department printed the story on the front page of the newspaper the telephone lines never stop ringing with a few complaints but most of the callers thanked us for a job well done. I telephoned my Mom to tell her that the investigation about the assassinations was over and to share the news that my story had been nominated for a Pulitzer Prize Award.

It's A Wonderful Day In The Neighborhood

I was sitting at my desk looking down at the crowded and busy New York streets savoring my survival and accomplishments when the telephone rang. The voice on the line was a voice I never thought I would hear from ever again or at least anytime soon. The voice on the line said hello Mr. Carter, I read your article and I must admit I'm impress that you kept it real and didn't sugarcoat the evil that these men committed. I answered thank you, how are you, and are you back from your trip? The Caller chuckled and answered that he wasn't back and that he would be taking and extended vacation in a country in South America where there wasn't any extradition treaty with the United States.

I told to the Caller that I'm going to assume that you are one of the Faith Leaders, and if so can I ask which one of them you are. The Caller chuckled again and stated that he needed to leave something for my imagination but he was confident that at some point I would figure it out. I ask the Caller what did he plan do with his life in South America? The Caller answered that his life didn't belong to him anymore, that it now belonged to Jesus Christ.

The Caller stated that there was a time when he and his colleagues thought that they were called by God to exterminate evil men but now he knows that he has been anointed by God to save lives, especially the lives of evil men. I asked the Caller if he was planning on becoming a preacher?

He answered that he was called and anointed by God the Holy Spirit to preach and teach the gospel and to help the poor. The Caller stated that he will miss our conversations and thanked me again for being patient and trusting him and said don't take any wooden nickels only plastic ones, the Caller chuckled, then I heard a dial tone...

New York City is one of the most visited city in the world and at the same time one of the most corrupt. Judges and politicians and other so-called public servants have allowed greed, and their uncheck (sexual) appetites, and self-interest to tarnish and destroy the reputation and trust that the public has placed in them. Some of the activities that these men participate in come from the darkest places in the human soul. But do not despair because here comes the Calvary. An anonymous group has vowed to clean up the city and exterminate these corrupt two-legged rodents who are wasting taxpayer's money. The group has made a vow to do whatever is necessary to make New Yorkers proud of their city again. This conflict is reminiscent of the battle between David and Goliath.

BIO

Author Isaac Gavin was born in South Carolina and currently resides in Massachusetts. He studied communications at Graham Junior College in Boston and journalism at the University of South Carolina. He has written two other books, "Thoughts Are Things", and "God Knows and God Speaks". This is his first novel, a fiction about corruption in New York City politics.

Made in the USA
Middletown, DE
07 November 2019